Praise for ***Sign in the Smoke***

"This brilliant young author has succeeded in crafting a suspenseful adventure story that will captivate audiences for years to come. Ganeshan continuously hits the spot with this heartwarming fantasy adventure that has many twists and turns. It will mesmerize audiences to the very last page. She delivers fascinating characters who continuously reveal their inner selves, and her intelligent dialog lets us into the minds of PowerSurge."

–Mr. Darrell Maskell

Shivani Ganeshan's 4th and 5th grade teacher, Quest Academy

"In this epic struggle between good and evil, extraordinarily bright students battle a band of secret witches who have controlled their world for centuries. Join the adventure of Olivia, Dash, Charles, and Vivian. This book is absolutely unforgettable."

–Mrs. Nancy Cohn

Shivani Ganeshan's Kindergarten teacher. Quest Academy

"Shivani Ganeshan is a talented, young writer. She has a unique ability to draw us into the fantasy world of PowerSurge. I can't wait to see what comes next. We will be talking about this gifted, young lady for years to come."

–Mrs. Janet Fricano

Shivani Ganeshan's Family Friend

"Olivia seems to be an ordinary 10-year-old, but there is a mystery surrounding her and her three best friends. Each of them has lost a parent to mysterious circumstances. They have banded together, calling themselves Powersurge. Olivia and her friends can't avoid the baffling events that surround them, and become enmeshed in a sinister world and a mystery that they must solve in order to save their families. *The Sign in the Smoke* is from a new, young author with a singular voice and an inventive imagination."

–Mrs. Becky Leff

Shivani Ganeshan's Fourth grade teacher. Quest Academy

"In the thrilling adventure, *The Sign In The Smoke*, ten-year-old Olivia must learn the secrets of her past to defeat an evil group of witches. Olivia and her friends face danger, solve puzzles, and outwit the problems of ordinary school. Shivani Ganeshan does an excellent job of creating wonderful characters. As we cheer for some and hope for the demise of others, this book will keep readers at the edge of their seats—and hoping for more books by this talented young author."

–Jane Kelley, author of *Nature Girl* and *The Girl Behind the Glass*

Dear Mrs. Leff,

Thank you so much for all of your help! I couldn't have done it without you.

with gratitude,
Shivani

SHIVANI GANESHAN

Dream Keepers Press

Published 2021 / Dream Keepers Press
Printed in the United States of America
(MOBI) E-ISBN: 978-1-950515-05-9
(EPUB) E-ISBN: ISBN-13: 978-1-950515-04-2
PRINT: ISBN-13: 978-1-950515-02-8

Library of Congress Control Number:
The Sign in the Smoke: written by Shivani Ganeshan
Edited by Jane Kelley
Interior Design by Caitlin Greer
Cover design by Caitlin Greer

Dedicated to my mom for helping me persevere throughout my journey and pushing me to never give up

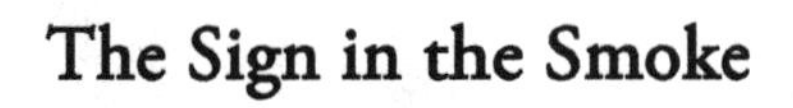

The Sign in the Smoke

1

It was just a few days into the new school year at Walter Bryce Academy. Teachers were in their classrooms, and students were hard at work. At least, that was how it was supposed to be, but for four fifth graders, the day would turn out very differently than how they had planned it.

"All right class, let's start with yesterday's homework. Does anybody have any questions?" asked Ms. B.

Ten-year-old Olivia Mendoza was stuck in another tedious class with her best friends. Charles, Dash, and Vivian were half asleep, as this was their first class of the day. Olivia's brown eyes, which were usually bright with enthusiasm, were half-closed, and her long, brown wavy hair was pulled into a sloppy ponytail. Olivia's dad had Mexican ancestry and was determined to teach Olivia to learn more about her heritage. Olivia was just a little taller than an average fifth grader. Unfortunately for her, the desks and chairs in the lower school science classroom were built for first graders, so her legs usually had red marks on them after class. Olivia picked a loose string off her turtleneck sweater. Even though it was almost the beginning of fall and the temperature was very warm, she always wore turtleneck sweaters. She had a determined look; some people were scared of her, even though she had a kind personality.

Olivia was a curious girl. If she had one wish, it would be to know who her mother was, and how she disappeared. However much she begged her dad to reveal the secret, he wouldn't budge. She spent many of her days daydreaming about her lost mother.

As usual, Olivia was deep in her thoughts, thinking about how much fun she would have that evening because she was going to the arcade with her best friends. They did almost everything together. That is, if they could make it through the boring school day. *I just want to sleep,* Olivia thought, bored out of her mind. She looked around the classroom. Kids were sitting on the dark-brown chairs, and most were leaning on the matching desks. Olivia's teacher, Ms. B., was standing in front of the room, her pointy nose facing the class as she glared at them in an unfriendly way. The floor featured black carpet with occasional rips and tears caused by children moving desks. The longest rips, however, were by the biggest desk in the front corner of the room, where Ms. B. sat. That was odd because the desk was too big for someone to lift; especially bony Ms. B. Olivia was seated behind Dash, who had just one person between him and the giant desk.

"Uh oh!" Dash whispered as he reached into his green backpack. "I think I left my homework on the bus. What am I going to do now?"

Olivia's eyelids had been drooping. She already knew what was being taught. Her dad had told her all about it a long time ago. But at the sound of Dash's voice, she jerked upright in her seat.

"I don't know. I guess you should just tell her," Olivia sighed, annoyed. Dash was always forgetting his homework, whether it was on the bus, at home, or it just completely slipped his mind. The year had barely begun and he had left his very first homework assignment on the school bus.

Dash Summers was an athletic boy with thick blonde hair and sky-blue eyes. His hair was thicker in the center and short on the sides. Ten-year-old Dash was a curious boy, and he was always ready to embark on a new adventure. He was the youngest of three, and he admired his older brother as his role model. He found his older sister annoying—even though she was the only girl in the Summers family. His mother had mysteriously died ten years earlier, right after he was born. It was still difficult for him to talk about her. He and Olivia often daydreamed together about how their moms would be. The absence of their mothers felt like a missing link in their life, and they always envied other kids who had both of their parents with them.

"So, we are looking at the *periodic table* here. Does anyone want to start us off by telling us their favorite element?" Ms. B. said, sweetly. "Let's see.... How about you, Dash, honey?"

"Uhhh. Umm," Dash stuttered. "Favorite element?" he whispered under his breath. He scratched his head and tilted it to the side. It's not like he wasn't smart, but Dash needed a specific style of teaching for him to remember things. Sometimes he would memorize a fact and then shoot a few hoops. Physical activity just helped him remember things better. He was always on the move.

Olivia leaned forward and whispered, "Just say silver."

Dash nodded and stopped scratching his head.

"Silver!" he answered, not understanding the question or his answer.

Dash was always speaking way too fast, and he never thought things through—at least, not the way Olivia did. She loved thinking, and would often get lost in her thoughts. Though she didn't know it yet, her bad habit would lead to terrible consequences. It always appeared as if she was daydreaming during classes, in her bed, and sometimes even when people were talking to her.

"I bet you guys didn't know that in ancient times, witches used silver to hypnotize people into doing what they wanted!" Charles exclaimed. They hypnotized people by…." He stopped abruptly.

Ms. B. had folded her arms and was glaring at Charles. "How do you know so much about witches?"

Charles shrugged. "I read." He returned her glare.

Ms. B. frowned. She quickly bent down to look at the floor and stood up again, looking relieved. "Well done, Mr. Williams. I guess." Ms. B. tapped her foot on the ground. "But next time don't interrupt me."

As she walked away, it looked to Olivia like she was still keeping an eye on Charles.

"Why is that?" Ms. B. asked Dash somewhat suspiciously, suddenly turning her attention back to him. "Why did you say silver?" She narrowed her cold, dark eyes. Ms. B. was a strict teacher, no doubt about that. She was always picking out children to embarrass during class. It was her way of keeping control. Olivia had a peculiar feeling about Ms. B. She was just… different. Odd, in a way.

"Um, shiny?" Dash said, shrugging his shoulders. He hoped that would satisfy Ms. B.

She raised her eyebrows and lightly shook her slender head, sighing deeply.

Olivia felt her eyelids close very slowly; she drifted into a light sleep. But it only lasted seconds before she heard a loud thump on her desk and jerked awake.

Ms. B. had banged her stiff hand on Olivia's desk. She was standing right over Olivia, staring into her eyes with a cold stare, making chills pass through Olivia's body.

"Wake up!" Ms. B. yelled. Her green necklace seemed to sparkle and create a luminous glow.

Olivia blinked. *It couldn't be!* she thought. *How is that possible?* There was something suspicious about Ms. B. She always seemed to be drinking mysterious concoctions, doing weird things, and saying things that weren't even words!

"Sorry." Olivia swallowed. She was a little intimidated by Ms. B., and that was very rare. Olivia was brave, ready to take on any challenge that came her way. She suddenly shuddered, feeling a cold vibe coming from Ms. B. The teacher carried a dark aura around her. Olivia was thankful she didn't have that quality herself.

"Now, who can tell me what the atomic symbol of silver is?" Ms. B.'s grayish-green eyes scanned the classroom as she walked back to the front. "Who *didn't* have their sleepy friend answer for them." She glared at Dash. He lowered his head.

One arm was waving so hard that it seemed to be about to fall off its owner's body.

"Charles, I know you know the answer, but let's give somebody else a try, how about that, sweetie?" Ms. B. said, sounding nice to cover up her irritaion.

Of course, Charles knew the answer. To Olivia, it seemed like he knew everything. Many other kids in the class called him smarty pants or teacher's pet, but Olivia actually admired him for his brains. Eleven-year-old Charles Williams was a very intelligent child. His mom was overprotective of him because he was all she had to remind herself of his father. Some people said he looked exactly like his father, with a golden tint to his brown hair, dark skin, and deep hazel eyes. He never bragged about being as intelligent as he was, and was very humble about all of his achievements.

"Do you know, Vivian?" Ms. B. asked, watching

Vivian's hand raise ever so slowly as if she wasn't sure if her answer was correct.

Poor, timid Vivian Zhao. She had no self-confidence; she hardly spoke to anybody but Charles, Olivia, and Dash. Charles was her cousin. Her blonde father was the brother of Charles's heartbroken mother. Vivian's mother grew up in Beijing, China, and Vivian often went there to visit her family. Charles's father had been from Nigeria, making the two cousins look quite different. Vivian looked like her mom, with light skin and brown eyes.

"Is it Au?" she asked nervously, shrugging her shoulders.

"Close, but no." Charles corrected his cousin. "That's the symbol for gold. The correct symbol for silver is Ag. Did you know that ancient people who lived in Turkey and Greece started mining for silver in 3000 BC? That's about 5,000 years ago. I wonder who discovered gold. Maybe it was the miner Jeo...?"

"That's enough, Charles." Ms. B.'s tone was harsh. Then her voice turned sweet again. "Now, students, does anyone else want to share their favorite element?"

"Dang it!" Dash whispered. He had dropped his pencil. He leaned down from his chair to pick it up. Then he stopped for a second while looking under Ms. B.'s desk.

Olivia didn't know what he saw under there, but from the look on his face, it was intriguing.

"Dash, sweetheart, is there a problem?" Ms. B. strolled across the classroom and tilted her pointed nose at Dash.

"No, nothing." He jerked back up into his seat, clenching his pencil so hard that it snapped. His wild blue eyes stayed fixed on the floor until he finally took a deep breath.

Olivia's dad had told her all about reading signs of emotion on someone's body. She could tell from Ms. B.'s menacing eyes that she didn't want Dash to see whatever was under her desk. *What could she be hiding?*

"Hey, Olivia, can I borrow a pencil?" Dash asked as he turned around.

"Sure." She reached into her pencil case. Leaning forward, she whispered, "What did you see under there?" Olivia really wanted to know what had surprised Dash so much.

"I'll tell you later. Charles and Vivian need to know too," he whispered back.

Millions of questions flitted in and out of Olivia's head. It wasn't like Dash to keep secrets. Usually, he couldn't hold anything in for more than a few seconds before spilling the news.

"Okay," Olivia said, with a confused expression on

her face. She passed a note to Charles, telling him that he needed to get them out of the class.

"All right, class. We are going to be learning about water today. Who can tell me what two elements make up water?" Ms. B. said.

Again, a hand was waving madly in the air. Of course, it belonged to Charles.

Olivia knew the answer as well. She wasn't afraid to be wrong. She raised her hand, confidently.

"Olivia?" Ms. B. called on her. "Do you have the answer?"

"It's hydrogen and oxygen."

Ms. B. gave Olivia an approving glance. That changed as soon as Charles started talking.

"That's correct," Charles said. "Did you know that we get our oxygen from trees? We breathe in oxygen, and we breathe out carbon dioxide in a fascinating process. The trees breathe in carbon dio...."

"Charles, I'll be seeing you after class, young man." Ms. B. was very angry that Charles had disobeyed her, even after she had given him a warning.

Many people would think Charles was showing off, trying to be the teacher. But Olivia knew he had other plans. *How did he think of that one?* Olivia wondered. *It's genius!*

"I'd rather not. English class is really fun, and I

have it next, so I'll think I'll skip staying after this time," Charles said rudely.

Olivia thought he was purposely trying to get in trouble. If she guessed correctly, it was all about the plan.

"Principal's office!" Ms. B. yelled. "Now!" She looked extremely angry like she was almost about to burst. She just wanted Charles to exit her classroom, so she could go on teaching the rest of the class. However, Charles's classmates were enjoying the scene; they were all snickering behind their books.

"Can I take my friends?" Charles asked. Olivia, Charles, Dash, and Vivian were a group of friends called PowerSurge. They did everything together, and never kept secrets from one another. At least, almost never.

"Of course not! What kind of teacher do you think I am? Just go!" Ms. B. screamed.

Charles shrugged, but he didn't move a muscle.

"I SAID, GO!"

Olivia could almost see smoke coming out of Ms. B.'s head. She wasn't sure if it was real or if it was her imagination. Then Olivia noticed something odd. Ms. B.'s eyes seemed to be turning a little bit red. Olivia looked away. This woman was creeping her out. She definitely wasn't normal. *Is she an alien?* Olivia thought.

No, of course not! What am I thinking?

The other kids in the room urged Charles to go by slightly nodding their heads towards the door. It seemed like all of a sudden they had gotten scared of Ms. B. After all, she might take out her anger on them.

Charles rolled his eyes and stubbornly crossed his arms.

Ms. B. threw her hands up in the air. "AARGH!" With that, Ms. B. stormed into the storage room that held all of the science equipment, probably to cool down. She slammed the door behind her so hard that the classroom floor shook.

Charles quickly gestured to Olivia, Dash, and Vivian to follow him as he maneuvered between desks to reach the classroom door.

Before he exited the room, Charles turned to the class and said sternly, "No one say a word, or you *will* regret it."

Their classmates looked at each other, debating whether or not they should tell the teacher.

Olivia sighed. It didn't matter. Ms. B. would notice immediately that they had left the class.

The four exited the room and breathed a sigh of relief. A few seconds later, they heard a stomping inside the classroom.

"Where did they go?" Ms. B.'s forcibly calm voice came from inside the room. "I said, where did they go? OH FOR HEAVEN'S SAKE, WHERE DID THEY GO?"

No response came. Knowing that Ms. B. would probably immediately check outside the door, PowerSurge started running.

They sprinted down the hallway of the school called the 'Hallway of Terror.' It wasn't necessarily scary. It was just old—really old. Some parts of the wall were peeling off, leaving dry paint hanging. The floor was made of tile, but many pieces were missing, and some were broken and scattered over the floor. There was only one piece of furniture; a couch that made Olivia dread walking down the Hallway of Terror. It was so dirty, Olivia thought that anyone who sat on it was crazy. It was so old that it was losing its color. It was so disgusting that, well, those details were unnecessary. Olivia was sure it had a stain for every color on the color wheel. It was once red with yellow flowers, but now it just looked brown with weird yellow splotches. One of the legs was missing, so it was leaning to the right. It looked like if someone sat on it, it would collapse within seconds. The kids in the school called it 'Grandma's couch.' After all, it did look like it was from the 1940s.

Olivia, Charles, Dash, and Vivian finally reached a safe spot in the dusty corner beside the door to the boys' bathroom. The rest of the hallway branched off from the corner, although it just led to a broken water fountain. Though Olivia usually didn't mind getting dirty, this was a different story. Dark green mold seeped through the cracks in the chipped tiles, that looked like they hadn't been tended to for at least ten years. Spider webs big and small lined the ceiling and corners of the area. *How can they even be allowed to keep a school with places like this?* Olivia squatted carefully to keep her body from touching the floor or the walls.

"Charles," Olivia exclaimed, as soon as she recovered from the run. "That was brilliant!"

"Yeah, but it got me into some serious trouble," he said, looking scornfully at a spider that was poised on the wall.

"What are you talking about?" Vivian asked. "Charles, I thought you hated English class." She narrowed her brown eyes.

"Well, Dash saw something, and I'm curious to know what it is," Olivia said.

Dash took a deep breath. "Hmm, lemme think." He teased Olivia. "I'll tell you if you buy me the new Babe Ruth pro card. Oh, and throw in a lollipop on top of that."

Olivia exhaled deeply and rolled her eyes. She reached into her pocket and sighed. "Don't do this to me, Dash!" She looked at him with an annoyed expression. "I'm running out of things to give you!"

He showed her his puppy-dog eyes.

Olivia laughed. "Fine. Just this time…here's a Twix." She threw a candy bar at Dash, hoping it would satisfy him. "Now, what did you see?"

Dash leaned in like he was about to tell them a scary story or an extremely juicy secret. "There was a book on the floor under her desk," he whispered excitedly.

Olivia glared at him. *Is that what I sacrificed my candy for?*

Charles let out an exasperated sigh. "Seriously?" he said. "I got into huge trouble just to hear THAT!"

"Let him finish," Vivian said, calming Charles down.

"The title was *A Guide to Witchcraft!*" Dash exclaimed. "And there was also a black cane with a skull and crossbones on it. And the weird thing is, when I looked at it, it started to move—like it sensed that I was watching it."

"What? No way!" The rest of the kids looked confused.

Suddenly, Charles's face lit up, like he had just come up with a huge invention that would change the world. "Don't you guys understand what that means? She's a witch!"

That wouldn't surprise me, Olivia thought, not really meaning it. "Witches aren't even real," Olivia said, thinking about her science teacher. "I mean, how?"

Her friends looked at each other.

"Of course she's a witch!" Dash exclaimed.

"Well, we can't assume that yet," Vivian said.

"Yeah, we need more proof." Olivia didn't want to make assumptions, even if she did think that what Dash saw *was* odd. *Maybe he thought he saw something that was just an ordinary book. But why would Ms. B. keep a book under her desk? I know she's weird, but who does that unless they're trying to hide it from someone?*

"Wait, guys?" Charles said. "If she is a witch, maybe that's why she was so interested in how I knew so much about witches!"

"And when she bent down right after that, she was probably checking under her desk," Dash exclaimed. "Just to make sure that Charles hadn't taken the book under there!"

"Well, I guess that makes sense," Olivia said. "But it's still not enough proof for me."

"Fine, but we should keep an eye on her," Dash said.

"Agreed," Vivian said. "I think she's going to be watching you, Dash, so be careful."

Dash nodded.

"I think we all have to be careful," Charles whispered.

2

"Who would like to grab some English books from the basement?" Mrs. Brody said. "I need four volunteers, please."

PowerSurge was stuck in another class, but none of them were paying attention. They were all thinking about what Dash had seen. They definitely didn't want to listen to Mrs. Brody ramble on about using punctuation in their writing.

"We can get them!" Dash volunteered, desperate for more time to talk about his discovery.

"Yes, that will do," Mrs. Brody said. She was a petite elderly woman, but that didn't mean she wasn't strict. Everyone was afraid of her stubbornness. She didn't accept any excuses, real or fake. "Go now, please."

The kids leaped out of their seats, eager to discuss Ms. B. in private.

"No running in the classroom!" Mrs. Brody yelled at Dash as he sprinted towards the door on the other side of the room. "Detention!"

What! Olivia thought. *For what?*

"B-b-but I," Dash stuttered. "Oh, well." He decided not to fight this battle. He didn't want to lose more valuable time by getting another detention for talking back.

"So," Olivia said, as they walked towards the basement. "Two of us got in trouble today, just to get some time to talk."

"It's fine," Dash said, speaking faster than normal. "We'll live. It's not like we lost Game 7 in the World Series by one run after a grand slam because our pitcher was injured and our substitute in the bullpen was terrible."

"Dash, say that in English please," Vivian said. "I know nothing about football!"

"That was so simple!" Dash threw his arms in the air. "Plus, it was baseball."

Vivian sighed and crossed her arms over her chest.

"Mrs. Brody was just in the mood to give a

detention," Olivia said sympathetically. "Unfortunately, you, Dash, were the unlucky victim."

"Sounds about right to me," Charles said. He walked down the basement stairs. When he got to the bottom, he stopped. "There are two doors," he said. "Which one should we take?"

"Duh!" said Dash. "The one we're not supposed to."

The kids in PowerSurge were such close friends because they shared so many connections. They each had one parent who had passed away. Their surviving parents had told them that Dash's mom, Vivian's dad, and Charles's dad had all died together. But no one ever said anything about Olivia's mom. Olivia and Dash were born at the same time in the same hospital, although Olivia didn't think their parents knew each other at the time. When they were two, Olivia and Dash met at a park. They had their first fight when Olivia claimed that Dash had "stolen her pinecone." The two became best friends after that. When Olivia and Vivian were four years old, they met at the Los Angeles airport. They bonded by watching movies on Olivia's dad's phone on the plane all the way home to Chicago. This friendship later led to Olivia and Dash meeting Charles, as he was Vivian's cousin. The four kids had been best friends ever since. PowerSurge was inseparable.

They all looked at the large, brown, wooden door with a nameplate marked: 'Private.'

Olivia exchanged nervous glances with Vivian. It was pretty obvious to Olivia that student were not supposed to see whatever was behind the door. *I'm not sure,* she thought. *It's probably marked private for a reason.*

"I don't know," Vivian said. "We really shouldn't." She liked to be cautious, stay out of trouble, and follow the rules. She definitely wasn't one of those annoying kids who snitched on others if they broke the rules. She was far from annoying; anyone who knew her well would agree.

"Yeah, it's probably locked anyway," Olivia said. "If it's worth exploring, the teachers won't leave it unlocked." She was a logical thinker.

"It's worth a try," Charles said. "Let's do it!" He pushed the door.

As Olivia had guessed, the door was locked.

"Aww, man," Dash said, putting his hands on his hips.

Vivian attempted to walk to the storage room. But she tripped over a bump in the carpet and fell. "Ouch!"

Olivia crouched down to help her up. She spotted

something shiny peeking out from under the fold in the carpet.

"Hey, that's probably the key!" Charles bent down and picked it up. "They must've hidden it under the carpet. That's why Vivian tripped!" He held the key next to the lock to see if it would unlock the door.

"No, don't open it!" Dash warned. "It's too simple. Nobody leaves a key right outside the room!"

Olivia opened her mouth, then closed it without speaking. This might be a trap, but she really wanted to know what was behind the door. She ignored her doubts. "I say we go in. We only want to see what's inside. It's not like we're going to take anything."

Her friends nodded in agreement.

Charles inserted the key into the lock and turned it. They heard a sharp click, and the door marked 'Private' was unlocked.

"Let's do it!" Vivian exclaimed.

Dash opened the door. What they saw inside made the kids' jaws drop. Lush, purple velvet couches were spread out in front of a giant flat-screen TV. The floor was covered with a comfortable gray carpet that added a cozy vibe to the room. A white marble island was covered with delicious snacks. A wooden shelf was full of really fun games. White bean bags were spread around the floor, matching the kitchen cabinets that surrounded the island on three sides. On one wall there was a giant painting of the ocean, depicting a monstrous wave. There were also many gaming consoles near the fireplace. A fire was burning inside, making a relaxing, crackling sound. Right beside it was an enormous hot tub with a jacuzzi.

"Of course the teachers don't want to share this with us!" Charles exclaimed. "How come we have to walk through places like the Hallway of Terror, but the teachers get *this*? No fair!"

"This place is awesome!" Dash yelled, as he picked up the remote to the TV. He seemed to have forgotten that he was at school and had a job to do.

Olivia slowly walked around the room, examining the distinct features of all the furniture. Then she stopped, intrigued by something.

"What's up Olivia?" Charles asked.

She was staring at the floor beneath a large plant in the back of the room. The plant was a beautiful, green stalk with bright red flowers in a white pot. It didn't fit in with the rest of the decor in the room. Underneath the pot was a square of bare wood, about two by two feet. This was the only part of the floor that didn't have carpet. She slowly and carefully approached it.

"What's that doing there?" she said. "It's so… random. I bet something's hiding under it." She reached around the pot and tried to move the plant, but it was way too heavy. "Guys, come help."

They rushed over.

"1,2,3...PUSH!" Vivian yelled.

They moved the plant off the square of wood.

"Hey, what's this?" Charles asked. He pointed to a small hinge on the edge of the wood square, almost covered by the carpet.

They bent down to examine it. It was a trapdoor! The opening was just large enough for a skinny adult.

Vivian frowned. "Okay, this is definitely a trap. Someone might want us to go down there."

Charles laughed. "Lighten up, Vivian. It's not like there's gonna be a monster waiting down there for us."

Vivian was still a little hesitant, but she shrugged. "There could be," she responded.

"I'll go first." Dash lifted the trapdoor and jumped into the opening.

"WHEEEE!" His voice echoed back up to them.

"My turn!" Olivia put her legs into the opening. She slid down a tunnel that seemed like it would never end. Eventually, her long legs touched the ground. She fell over onto something oddly shaped. It was moving!

"Hey!" Dash yelled. "That's me!"

"Sorry," she said, holding in a laugh. She scrambled up onto her feet. "What is this place?"

Vivian screamed as she came sliding down the tunnel.

A few seconds later, Charles appeared. "Is there a light switch anywhere?" His arms slid across the wall feeling for a light switch. "Aha!" he yelled. He flicked on the lights.

Olivia's senses came flooding back to her. She was standing in a dark hallway that was barely the height of a full-grown woman. The hallway led to only one room, with no other doors. PowerSurge walked forward and entered a large room. It had a scary aura to it, because most of the room was black. There were no windows or any hint of the outside world. The desk in the center of the room was one of the few brown items. Its edges were lined with rounded golden pearls. Olivia could see the reflection of her astonished face on the small surface of each shiny pearl. Sitting on the desk was a nameplate that read "Agatha Black." There were many paintings on the walls portraying women dressed in black. The largest one depicted someone in a jet-black mask that covered his or her face. There were cobwebs in the corners of the room. A mirror was hanging on one wall, adding a very chilling touch. Its black border had weird designs. The mirror looked recently polished. Olivia noticed a green necklace hanging from one of the many hooks on the wall. She couldn't quite remember where she had seen the necklace before. On the far side of the room was a dusty wooden bookshelf. It was painted black, exactly like the rest of the room. Many books were on it. Olivia was surprised that most of their titles involved witchcraft. She took a book off the tall shelf. It was titled, *A History of Witchcraft*. Olivia slowly opened it. She almost dropped it when it started talking to her.

"*Hello, hello, my curious friend. Here the story will begin. But beware as....*"

"Nope," Olivia mumbled as she slammed the book shut and hastily threw it back on the shelf. *A book that can talk?* she wondered. *What is this place?* She turned to her friends. "Let's get out of here. Quick!"

"We shouldn't be here!" Vivian exclaimed. "We're going to get in serious trouble! We don't even know what this place is, how it's here, who created it, or exactly what we're doing here."

The boys were grinning and skipping around the room.

"Guys," Dash exclaimed as he pointed to a cane, half-hidden by the bookshelf. "That's the cane that I saw under Ms. B.'s desk! She must have been down here recently!"

Olivia stepped closer to the cane. *No way! So maybe Ms. B. isn't normal! I knew it!* She examined the cane inquisitively. It was jet black, with small carvings of skull and crossbones, just as Dash had described it.

"Oh yeah, that's who this necklace belongs to!" Olivia said, rushing to the green necklace she had seen on the wall earlier. "Ms. B.!"

"No way!" Charles exclaimed. "Do you think this place has something to do with Ms. B.?"

"It's possible," said Vivian. "As far as I know, none of the other teachers are…spooky enough to make a room like this."

"She must've been trying to hide the cane behind the bookshelf, but then she rushed out of here," Olivia said. "Maybe the new period was starting."

Dash nodded. "We should come back here some other time to investigate. There's a lot of info we need to fill in the blanks."

"No," Olivia said. "We can't come back here! It's too dangerous! We don't want to be caught." She reached in her pocket and pulled out her phone. She took pictures of everything in sight. After two minutes, she was satisfied with the quality of her photographs.

"Olivia, great idea!" Charles exclaimed. "But Mrs. Brody will get suspicious soon if we don't bring back those textbooks."

Dash immediately turned, expecting to find the door out of the weird room. He was faced with a plain wall. "Huh, where did the door go?" He looked around for a way to get out of the room. There was nothing. "It was just here! I know we came through it!"

"I knew it was a trap! Someone must have set this up," Vivian said. "How are we going to get out now?"

"Relax, Viv. Let's just look around." Charles reassured his cousin.

PowerSurge started searching everywhere.

"How does this Agatha Black person get out of here?" Dash asked curiously. "She *has* to be a witch. That would explain the talking book. She can probably just teleport or fly out of here!"

"But we can't teleport," Vivian said. "Or fly. Does that mean we're stuck here forever?"

Olivia shook her head. "There has to be *some* secret passage that leads back up. What if Agatha ran out of magic here? If that's possible. She would need some way to get back up without using her powers."

Olivia kept looking, hoping there would be something in sight.

"Hey, what's this?" Dash asked. He was staring at a red button next to the TV on the wall. "Should I press it?" He put his finger on the red surface of the button.

"No!" Charles exclaimed, lunging towards Dash.

By surprise, Dash accidentally leaned on the button and pressed.

Olivia barely had time to think before she was flung

up in the air. It took about three seconds before she realized that she and her friends were standing in front of the potted plant in the teachers' lounge.

"Well, that just happened," Vivian said sarcastically.

"Weird, right?" Olivia checked to make sure all of her limbs were still attached to her body. Eager to get out of the teachers' lounge, PowerSurge entered the room marked 'Storage,' quickly grabbed the English textbooks, and raced back to the classroom.

"What took so long?" asked Mrs. Brody. "You were gone for ten minutes. You shouldn't have been. You aren't old and wobbly on your feet like me. We were waiting." She had one of those I-know-what-you've-been-up-to looks on her face.

Olivia avoided her gaze.

"There were so many books to choose from," Charles lied. He snickered as he glanced at his friends.

Mrs. Brody sighed. "Children these days," she muttered. "In the old days, they wouldn't tolerate any dilly dally. I really should think about retiring."

Please do, that would be nice, Olivia thought. She smiled guiltily at Mrs. Brody.

Mrs. Brody looked at her, confused, then she shook her head and grabbed the textbooks from their hands.

English was the last thing on their minds as PowerSurge wondered what their experience in the teachers' lounge meant. All four of the children now knew they had just gotten themselves involved in something serious. Should they forget what they had seen? Should they keep it a secret? Whatever they chose, it had to be the right decision.

3

After a few minutes, which seemed like years to the kids, a bell rang. It was time for recess and lunch. The class rushed out the door to the playground. PowerSurge headed for their usual spot, the bench that was farthest from the play equipment. They always sat there so they could talk privately. However, as soon as they sat down, the school bullies came up to them.

"Oh, it's CowerSurge," sneered their leader, Hawk.

Ugh, not them again! Olivia thought. *I wish they would leave us alone. They should find other kids to pick on! We're not the least bit afraid of them!*

They mainly bullied Charles because he was so smart.

"Too scared to do anything except answer questions," Blaze said.

"More like, too *busy* to sign autographs," Charles retorted, unfazed. "Off you go. This genius does not have time for crazy fans like you three."

Hawk widened his eyes and walked away, motioning for his friends to follow him.

"Next time I'll take notes," Dash said as he slapped Charles on the back. "That was pretty good, mate."

"All right, all right, that *was* good, but back to work," Olivia said. She opened the photos she had taken earlier of Ms. B.'s hideout. "What can we make of this?"

"Well, this Agatha Black is obviously a witch of some kind, but why is her hideout under our school?" Charles asked.

"That's the last place people would look?" Vivian said.

Olivia quickly jotted that down with her matching purple pen. A thought rushed into her head. "Agatha Black, with a *B*, you guys. What if this is Ms. B. we're talking about here?"

"That might be why the yearbook never says Ms. B.'s first name," Charles said.

"Of course!" Vivian's face lit up. "Let's ask her!"

"Are you kidding?" Dash looked at her like she was

stupid. "You want us to just walk up to her and say, 'Hey, Ms. B., we were just wondering, are you a witch?'"

"Of course not," Vivian said, looking offended. "I was saying that we should set some sort of trap that could prove she is a witch. We know she visits the basement."

"You guys, I'm pretty sure witches always wear gloves because they don't have fingernails," Charles said. "We always wondered why Ms. B. always wears gloves, even when it's not winter!"

Olivia frowned in disgust at the thought of someone not having fingernails. Although, Charles's thought *did* make sense. "You could be right Charles," Olivia said. "But we should probably get some more evidence. Just to be sure."

"Evidence, schmevidence," Dash said, annoyed. "Let's just go confront her. What more evidence do we need? Be realistic, Olivia."

"No, Dash, you be realistic," Vivian said. "We can't just accuse someone of being a witch. No one would believe us. Besides, if Ms. B. is *actually* a witch, we'd most likely be dead before...."

The bell rang, interrupting Vivian. It was time for lunch. Olivia was grateful she didn't have to hear the end of Vivian's sentence.

"Let's see if we can find a table that's close to Ms. B.," Dash suggested.

They ran inside the noisy lunchroom and looked around for her.

"She's not here," Charles said disappointedly.

"Maybe she is in her office in the basement?" Vivian said.

"It's possible!" Dash said. "I thought we weren't returning there, but let's go!"

The kids snuck around Mr. Jentzen, who was reluctantly watching the fifth graders eat lunch. He was chewing with his mouth open and was making a lot of noise. Olivia winced.

PowerSurge ran to the basement. They were surprised to find it was still unlocked.

"Wait," Olivia said, before they opened the door. "It's lunch break right now. Don't you know that off-duty teachers usually eat lunch in the teachers' lounge?"

"I'm not so sure," Vivian said. "Some teachers like to eat in their classrooms so they can multitask and do their work while they have lunch. In fact, most of them do. Maybe we should check a couple classrooms to see if there are teachers inside."

"Good thinking, both of you," Charles said. "But I don't think we have time to go upstairs and check some classrooms. I guess it's just a risk we'll have to take."

Olivia slowly turned that handle and opened the door. She peeked through the crack in the door.

The music teacher, Mr. Berry, was sitting on the large, velvet couch facing 90 degrees away from them. He had the TV on full blast, so any sound the children made would be drowned out by that. Seated beside him was Ms. Mullins, the young drama teacher. Olivia and her friends slowly opened the door and sneaked in. Olivia cringed at the loud creaking noise. *Did they hear that?*

Mr. Berry and Ms. Mullins showed no sign that they had heard the noise and kept on watching their TV program about Mozart. After a couple of seconds, Ms. Mullins got up to use the bathroom. Olivia, Dash, Charles, and Vivian quickly ran out of the room and partially closed the door. They waited outside the entrance to the lounge until Ms. Mullins had safely closed the bathroom door behind her. Entering the room again, PowerSurge got down on their hands and knees and quietly scampered to the other side of the room. However, as soon as they touched the plant, Mr. Berry stood up to get some more pizza from the open box on the kitchen bar. Dash quickly grabbed Olivia's hand and pulled her behind a large leather couch that was facing away from Mr. Berry. Charles and Vivian dove under a table piled high with books. But they were too late. Mr. Berry had already turned and spotted them.

"Charles? Vivian?" he asked, with a puzzled look. "What are you doing here?"

"I…er…I lost my phone," Charles lied, stuffing his hands in his pockets. He looked around for Dash and Olivia to make sure they were still safely hidden from Mr. Berry's sight.

"Well, I don't know what made you think that it would be here," Mr. Berry said as he frowned in disapproval. "Go now, and don't come again. This room is for teachers only. You weren't supposed to be here in the first place."

They were lucky that Mr. Berry was the teacher who caught them because he didn't take everything as seriously as some other teachers. *I'm glad it wasn't Ms. B. or Mrs. Brody who caught us!* Olivia thought. *We'd all be in the principal's office right now!*

As Vivian and Charles made their way towards the door, Vivian ran her fingers across her forehead. Olivia knew she did this whenever she had an idea.

Vivian whispered something into Charles's ear. He grinned, reached into his pocket, and looked around to make sure that Mr. Berry wasn't watching them. They walked out the door and turned the corner. However, when Mr. Berry was about to shut the door, Charles quickly shoved a penny in the lock to prevent it from locking. Thankfully, Mr. Berry didn't realize what had happened and sat back down on the couch. Charles and Vivian snuck back in and joined Dash and Olivia in their hiding spot.

"That could've gone very wrong," whispered Dash, as he shifted his balance from one foot to the other.

"Let's go on," Vivian said. "Lunch break will end soon if we don't hurry up."

PowerSurge still had to move the plant to get through the trapdoor. Communicating just by nodding and gesturing, Olivia and her friends grabbed the plant and pushed it to one side. But just as they thought that they could enter the trap door, the plant tilted a bit too much. It was about to tip over when Charles and Dash quickly reached out and held it. They weren't strong enough to push it back up, even with the help of Vivian and Olivia.

"Go through the trapdoor," Dash whispered, squinting as he used all of his strength to help Charles keep the plant from falling. "We'll follow you."

How much dirt is in this plant? Olivia thought. *It's so heavy!*

Olivia and Vivian nodded in agreement and slid through the trapdoor. This time, they had to be extremely quiet; they definitely didn't want Mr. Berry to catch them again. Even though she was sliding down the chute for the second time, Olivia still felt a thrill as the humid wind rushed against her face. She squinted, so her eyes wouldn't sting. Once Vivian and Olivia were safe in the hallway, they stood up and waited for Charles and Dash to arrive. The faint sound of pottery breaking far above was followed by the thump of Charles and Dash reaching the hallway. They scrambled to their feet and looked around.

Before Olivia could take a step forward, she froze at the sound of talking in Agatha's office.

"Guys, be quiet," Olivia warned. "I think someone's in there!"

They slowly crept towards Ms. B.'s office with Olivia in the lead. Olivia peeked in the doorway and her heart stopped for a second. Someone was talking! *It was Ms. B.!*

"It's her!" she whispered. "Ms. B. is in there, talking to one of the pictures on the wall?"

The kids exchanged confused looks.

"Why would she be talking to a picture?" Charles asked. "That doesn't make sense. Maybe she's talking on the phone or something."

Olivia shook her head. "Nope, definitely not on the phone. She has to be talking to a picture. She's staring right at the biggest one. Eye contact and everything."

"Well, if our theory that Ms. B. is a witch is correct, then it wouldn't be odd that she can use magic to talk to people in pictures," Vivian said.

"We never thought of this, but it's possible that Ms. B. is a good witch," Dash said. "I mean, she is a teacher after all. Maybe she's trying to help us?"

Olivia had never heard of a good witch, but it was an okay theory.

Suddenly, they heard another loud voice inside the office. It was the person Ms. B. was talking to. The voice was deep and hollow, making Olivia think of a bottomless pit. The picture that seemed to captivate Ms. B.'s attention the most was the biggest one in the center of the wall. The photo was in a thick, wooden frame, painted with sleek, dark black. It seemed like the person in the picture was moving, but that could've just been Olivia's imagination. Olivia had an odd feeling about the voice of the person in the picture—almost like she recognized it.

"Don't forget to take him without being seen," the voice warned. "The man in the household is potentially dangerous to our mission. He's one of the only people who can stop us."

Olivia glanced at her friends. *Take him?* she wondered. *Take who? Which man?*

"Yes, I know, boss," Ms. B. said. "I shall kidnap

him, but keep him alive. Unfortunately, I cannot kill him because he is of use to us if we want this mission to be successful. But don't worry, he will not be living under great circumstances." She smiled evilly.

"Good. The eviler the better." The voice cackled.

Vivian couldn't help gasping in fright.

Ms. B. spun her chair to face the hallway. "Hold on, Master Agnes," she growled. "I thought I heard something outside. Let me check."

She stood up and walked toward the hallway—right towards PowerSurge!

"Never mind her being a good witch." Dash corrected his previous theory.

"In other words, we're done for!" Vivian whispered.

4

"Not if I can help it," Olivia said. She was exactly like her dad. She never gave up easily, and neither did he. She quickly devised a plan in her head. *Is it going to work?* She questioned her own plan. *We have no choice but to try.*

Olivia reached into her pocket and pulled out a small bouncy ball she had won at the arcade a few weeks ago. She prepared to throw it from behind the door. As Ms. B. started to pass through the doorway, Olivia flung the ball along the hallway.

Ms. B. rushed towards the ball. While she examined it, her back was to the kids.

Olivia quickly led her friends into the office.

"What?" Ms. B. asked, looking around. "Who's there?" She walked further down the hallway, expecting to find people there.

Olivia breathed in relief. *It worked!* As she was throwing the ball, Olivia had been scared that Ms. B. would look for the source of the ball instead of at the ball itself. Thankfully, she hadn't looked for Olivia and her friends. Now PowerSurge needed a place to hide before Ms. B. came back.

Olivia crept towards the bookshelf and signaled for the others to follow her. They put their hands against the bookshelf and pushed. The bookshelf didn't move. From the hall, they heard footsteps getting louder. Ms. B. was approaching.

"Guys, PUSH!" Dash whispered.

They pushed so hard that Olivia was sure the bookshelf would move. But, to her surprise, it stayed there. *Come on! We're going to be caught now!* Olivia thought.

"Guys, this isn't going to work!" Vivian whispered. "We have to try something different."

Olivia looked around the room. The black cane hanging on the wall caught her attention. Olivia pulled it off its hook. She felt as if an electric shock passed through her body. The cane was heavier than she thought. She tapped the bookshelf with it. To her surprise, the shelf moved! *Why did that work?* Olivia wondered. *I'm not a witch. How did the magic work for me?* Dash frowned at her. Olivia realized that he had touched the cane in their previous visit to the office, but nothing happened. Olivia's confusion was intensifying.

The space was just large enough for the children to crawl through. Olivia put the cane back on the hook and sat on the floor beside her friends. There was a large tunnel behind the bookshelf that led into the darkness. Olivia wondered what it led to. She thought she heard something that sounded like a whisper coming from the other side. She was about to go in deeper.

PowerSurge wanted to know where the tunnel led, but they were even more curious about what Ms. B. was up to.

Will she notice that the bookshelf has been moved? Olivia wondered.

Vivian gave her a silent high five for thinking of using the cane.

"What do you think she's doing now?" asked Dash, who was next to Charles.

The chair squeaked as Ms. B. sat in it. "Sorry, Master." She let out a wicked cackle. "The children will be dead by morning. Nothing will prevent us from gaining absolute power." She let out another cackle and ended the call.

Olivia suddenly realized that her life might be in danger. Would she be dead by morning? She was a very brave girl, but her life had never been threatened before. For the first time, she was really scared.

PowerSurge exchanged worried looks. They all had the same question in their minds.

Finally, Vivian whispered that thought. "Is she talking about us?"

Dash stood up. His head was barely a centimeter below the ceiling of the tunnel. "I'm going to go out and show that woman what we're made of." He was obviously expressing his fear by showing anger towards Ms. B.

Charles and Olivia pulled his hands and forced him to sit down.

"Are you stupid?" Olivia whispered. "You'll ruin our chances of ever defeating these witches." After she said this, she noticed that Vivian was looking downcast. "What's the matter, Vivian?"

"Nothing," Vivian whispered. "It's just...Max would have known what to do."

Max was Vivian's brother who had disappeared nearly two years ago. Vivian still hadn't given up hope that he was alive, even after his funeral. It was strange that they paid their last respects to an empty coffin. Max was only two years older than Vivian, and he was really fun to hang out with. Olivia missed him a lot. She didn't have any siblings, and Max had been like an older brother to her. She sometimes wondered why the search party that looked for Max had found no trace of him whatsoever. Tears started running down Vivian's face. Olivia hugged her. She would always be there for her friends, no matter what. Olivia started crying with her when suddenly she heard a phone ring. As she peeked out, she realized that it wasn't Ms. B.'s. It was Charles's! She held in a gasp. *No!* They would certainly be caught now. Sure enough, she was right.

Ms. B. approached the bookshelf they were hiding behind. Charles shut off his phone, but it was too late now. The dark, skinny, tall shadow of Ms. B. towered mightily over the children's heads and engulfed them in darkness.

"Well, well, well," she cackled. "What have we here?"

It's over now! There's no way she'll let us go, Olivia thought. She had never seen her friends look so terrified before. She was just as aghast, but she wasn't going to show Ms. B. that she was frightened.

Olivia stood up. "Who do you think you are?" she asked. "If you think that you can kill us that easily, then you are even more stupid than I thought." Olivia was usually a polite girl. She would never show this sort of disrespect to anyone, especially a teacher. But this was an exception.

Ms. B. smiled evilly and stared into Olivia's eyes, searching for the fear that Olivia was hiding.

This is so scary! Olivia thought. *What's she going to do to us?* Right now, if her theory was correct, she was fighting for her friends' lives—and her own. She looked at her friends for some backup.

Dash hesitantly stood up. Instead of the small, scared tone that Ms. B. was expecting, he spoke with a determined voice. "You and your *master* will be dead by tomorrow—not us!"

"Clever little children," Ms. B. said. "However, knowing the capital of Tanzania won't get you anywhere in this world. Not that I care."

"By the way, it's Dodoma." Charles spoke up from his spot next to Vivian. Then, he stood up beside Dash. "Let us out of here!"

"I don't think so," Ms. B. chuckled. "You'll be here until you're nothing more than a squashed pile of bones."

What does that mean? Olivia thought. She kept her eyes on Ms. B. as the other kids exchanged worried glances.

Finally, Vivian stood up. "I bet you can't," she contradicted. "We're a lot smarter than you think, Ms.

B. Or should I call you Agatha?"

Olivia had no idea that Vivian had enough courage to say something like that.

Agatha clenched her fists and revealed her rage. Her eyes turned bloodshot and became bright red.

Olivia tried to look away as it was freaking her out. *She's definitely not normal!* Olivia thought.

"We are PowerSurge!" the kids chorused.

"We'll see about that." Agatha laughed. "Stupid children," she growled under her breath. Without another word, she turned on her heels and started to leave the room. She looked back at them. "You know what? Let's play a game. I'll give you a chance to escape, just so you can see how stupid you really are. You'll never get out. Have fun with this, children." She cackled and disappeared into mid-air.

Suddenly, they were alone. PowerSurge immediately scattered, looking for clues that might somehow lead them outside of the dark office. Olivia looked around. The button that had gotten them out last time was gone, and so was the door to the hallway. They were stuck.

After minutes of searching, Charles spoke up. "Guys, come here. Look at this." He was standing right by an old, rusty-looking couch. He had lifted one of the cushions and there was a tiny note there. The note read,

'I have hands but cannot clap. I have a face, but I cannot smile. What am I?'

"Isn't it obvious?" Vivian asked. "Max must have told me this riddle a billion times before he disappeared."

They all looked at her, confused.

"It's a clock!" she shouted.

"Ohhh," Dash said. He looked around the room. He pointed to a shiny clock hanging on the wall.

The kids ran to it and reached up as far as they could, but it was just a foot above their reach.

"It's too high," complained Charles. He crouched down and Olivia sat on his shoulders. He stood up and Olivia took the clock off the wall and gently handed it to Dash. He ran to Agatha's desk and turned it over.

There was another piece of paper taped onto the back. He read it out loud. "*I'm tall when I'm young, and I'm short when I'm old. What am I?*" he read. "Huh? What could it be? Guys, come help!"

"Let's try looking around the room," Vivian said.

Suddenly, Dash called his friends over. "I've got it!" he yelled. "It's a flower!"

"That makes sense, but I don't see any flowers in here," Charles said, after looking around. "Good try, though," he added after seeing the disappointed look on Dash's face.

This place sure could use flowers, Olivia thought.

PowerSurge kept on looking, determined to find their way out of the dark office.

Olivia stopped in front of Ms. B.'s desk when she noticed something that fit the description in the riddle.

"Guys!" she yelled. "Over here!" When they had all gathered around her, she said, "It's a candle!"

A large lit candle gave off a faint light. Wax dripped down the sides of the candle and formed a sticky pool around its base.

Dash lifted the candle off the desk. Vivian peeled the riddle off the plate it was on. She read it out loud. "*I stay where I am when I go off. What am I?*"

PowerSurge immediately looked around the room again. Nobody found anything. Minutes later, they still had not solved the riddle.

Olivia wondered if there was a time limit to this escape room. She thought that if there was, they had probably already exceeded it.

All of a sudden, Dash's face lit up. "I've got it!" he exclaimed.

Please be right! Olivia thought. *I want to get out of here!*

"What is it?" Vivian asked, as she came over to look at what he was bending over.

"It's an alarm clock!" Dash shouted. He picked up a

bright red old-fashioned alarm clock.

Olivia wondered why she hadn't noticed it earlier, as it contrasted the rest of the interior of the room greatly. It was turned on and it seemed like it was counting down to something.

Charles stepped forward. "Why didn't we just look at this alarm clock instead of the clock hanging off of the wall?" he asked. "We could have saved ourselves a lot of time."

Of course! Olivia thought. *Now I kind of wish we had made a mistake.* "Speaking of time," she said. "What if that clock is counting down the time we have left in here?"

"That makes sense," Dash said. "We should get going. There are only ten minutes left on the clock." He glanced at its face with a worried look.

Charles came to him and read the riddle out loud.

"*I get wet when I dry. What am I?"* he read.

There were a couple of minutes of silence while the kids were thinking. They looked at Charles since he was great at riddles.

"Let's look at this one logically. What dries things?" he asked.

The sun? Ideas passed through Olivia's head as she thought of possible answers to the riddle. "A towel!" Olivia exclaimed. She looked around the room and pointed. "There's one over there!"

Dash picked up a brown towel from the shiny surface of Agatha's desk. Olivia glanced at the clock. They had one minute left. She ran to Dash's side and helped him search the towel for another riddle or a key.

"Here!" she exclaimed. To her relief, it was a key they found taped to the towel, not another riddle. *Finally!* She yanked the key off the towel and ran to the door of the office, which had just appeared but was still locked.

"Twenty seconds," Vivian warned.

Olivia and Dash fidgeted with the lock and key, but they couldn't open it.

"Ten seconds left," Charles said.

Olivia was desperate to get out of this place with no connection to the outer world.

"Five…four…." Vivian counted.

Dash desperately tried different ways of trying to open the door. "Three…two…." Nothing happened. "One second!"

A click sounded and the door opened. They sped out of the door.

"Yes! Nice job, guys!" Dash exclaimed. "Hey, Charles!" Dash looked around. "Wait a minute, where's Charles?"

They looked back. Charles was stuck in the room.

He hadn't gotten out fast enough. The worst part was that the walls in the office were slowly coming together. If Charles didn't get out within seconds, he would be squashed into a pancake.

"Charles, move!" Vivian shouted. She held her arm out for Charles to grab, but he was too far away.

"I can't!" Charles breathed. "I'm stuck!" He desperately tried to move, but he just couldn't budge.

"Why can't you move?" Olivia asked frantically.

"I think my shoe is stuck on some sort of glue puddle," Charles shouted. "Agatha must've put it on the floor!"

"We'll get you out," Dash said. He held one of Charles's hands. Vivian and Olivia held the other. The walls were approaching. They tugged, but he didn't move.

"I feel a little bit looser!" Charles exclaimed. "Try again."

They pulled again, but Charles still got only a little looser. Now the walls were about to hit him. They were inches away from touching the ends of his stuck shoe.

He has to come out! Olivia thought.

Olivia, Vivian, and Dash pulled once more. Charles came flying toward them. As he moved, his glasses flew off his face and fell into the office. PowerSurge watched as the walls touched together and the glasses broke with a sickening crunch.

"That would have been me if you hadn't gotten me out," Charles said gratefully. "We should get going. I can't really see, but I'm pretty sure that if I looked at my watch, it would tell me that we have missed the fourth period."

"Hey, did you guys notice how the walls just passed through Agatha's things and didn't even damage them one bit?" Dash asked. "That means that these witches are magic experts. We'd better be careful."

"Yeah," Vivian agreed. "The walls opened back up and all of the things look good as new."

The kids turned their backs on Agatha's office. They walked away, vowing to never return. However, Olivia knew that Agatha would be back the next day, ready to try to kill them. What they didn't know was that she would be back with vengeance…and sooner than PowerSurge expected.

5

"If we want to get to the bottom of this so-called Ms. B., then we'll have to skip the arcade," Dash said. "I hate to say it, but investigating her will probably be more fun."

PowerSurge was walking home from school. They were heading to Charles's house. They always went to one house for a couple of hours after school to do homework together. They didn't share all of their classes, but when they did, they worked on their homework with each other.

"Should we tell the police?" Vivian asked, tightening her backpack straps around her shoulders.

How could she think that! Olivia thought. *The*

witches would definitely kill us then!

Dash jerked to a stop, his eyes wide. "We can't do that!" he exclaimed. "Agatha will kill us! Literally!"

"I know," Vivian said. "But it's a lot more dangerous if we investigate ourselves."

The kids walked past a broken-down railroad that signified that they were almost at Charles's house. The sign outside read *Oak Transport* in rusty letters. Bright yellow caution tape blocked people from entering the old and eerily-built place. Olivia often wondered what lay behind that caution tape, but she never tried to pass it.

"We could bike back to school and do some more investigating," Charles said. "But you guys would have to get your bikes from your houses. Plus, that might be a bit too dangerous."

Olivia wanted to call her dad. He always had great ideas about what to do. Though he had been acting strange lately, Olivia still thought his bubbly personality would still provide him with great ideas. "I'll ask my dad what to do," Olivia said. "He'll know something fun."

PowerSurge agreed on this and decided to skip the arcade.

Five minutes later, Olivia jumped on Charles's bed. Dash sat beside her, Vivian sat on one of Charles's beanbags, and Charles took his place on the chair that belonged to his desk. Olivia's phone vibrated and she picked it up. Her dad had texted her back. She read the message out to her friends.

"Try exploring Oak Transport," she read aloud. "You'll find some cool stuff. I went there when I was a kid." Olivia was not sure her friends were up to this. Dash looked excited. Charles looked like he was a little reluctant, but was willing to go anyway. However, Vivian looked like she would need a lot of convincing to go.

"I'm not sure," Vivian said. "There could be really bad things down there. For example, dangerous people."

Olivia agreed with her, but she was quite a daredevil, and she wanted to go on an exciting adventure. "We'll be fine. We just need some things to protect us." Olivia began to think of what items they might need.

"We're probably going to have to make a trip to each of our houses before we can go because we're going to need a lot of things," Charles said, as he uncapped the pen that was attached to his notepad.

"Okay, so the first thing we'll need is one flashlight each," Vivian said. "We should probably take extra batteries too."

Charles quickly jotted that down.

"We'll need snacks," Dash said. "Don't forget about those!"

"Let's take our mega-dart nerf guns," Olivia said. "They hurt if you get hit by one."

Charles wrote that down. "Let's take night binoculars too." He wrote down his own suggestion.

"And walkie-talkies in case we get separated," Olivia said. "I have a four-way connector."

"Bring a sweatshirt too," Charles said. "We don't know how cold it may be inside."

"That should be it," Dash said. "And don't forget your color codes."

PowerSurge had secret code names for each other. They were each a color. Olivia was purple, Dash was green, Charles was blue, and Vivian was pink. The kids ran to Charles's garage.

"How are we going to do this?" Dash asked. "We have one bike and four people."

"I have an idea," Vivian said. "Dash and Olivia can go to their houses together because they live in the same neighborhood. Charles can take me to my house, and then we can meet back here. If we stick together, we'll be safer."

"Sounds good," Olivia said. She and Dash set off to their neighborhood. When they got to Olivia's house, she entered the garage code. Then she and Dash went inside the house.

Olivia's dad, who was an archaeologist, was sitting on a couch with his legs propped up on a stool. He was watching TV and he had a bowl of chips in one arm. His other arm was petting Olivia's dog, Magnus. Magnus was an Alaskan Husky. He was named after the Latin stem *magn*, meaning large. He was still a puppy, but, as the name suggested, he would grow to be very big. He would be a little heavier than Olivia, and she could almost ride him like a horse. As soon as Magnus he saw Olivia, he ran towards her. She rubbed him in his favorite spot—behind his ears.

Olivia's dad turned around to greet them. "Hi, Olivia. What are you doing here? Didn't you get my text to explore Oak Transport?"

Olivia was surprised her dad hadn't figured out why they were at her house. "We need to pack for our adventure," she said. "We don't know what's down there." Her dad seemed to be getting very forgetful in the last couple of weeks. It wasn't his age that was causing his loss of memory because he was only 39 years old. It was like something was troubling him. His mind was probably on something important that he wasn't prepared to share with Olivia.

"Oh, yeah, right," Olivia's dad said. "Good thinking."

"I thought you went there when you were younger," Olivia said. "Don't you remember?"

Olivia's dad noticed Dash standing next to her. "Hello Dash," he said, ignoring Olivia's question. "Are you here to gather materials as well?"

Dash looked very surprised. Olivia's dad usually didn't ask why her friends were at her house. "Uh. Well…I'm…." Suddenly, Dash couldn't remember what he was doing at Olivia's house.

"Dad." Olivia sat next to him. "Are you feeling okay?" But her dad didn't answer. His eyes were glued to the TV, even though it was on a random commercial break.

He stayed like that for about ten seconds. Then he jerked his head towards Olivia and Dash. "Well, go already!" he yelled. "Just leave me alone!"

"Olivia, c'mon!" Dash whispered urgently.

Olivia followed him to her room, away from her dad. She was still deeply concerned about him, because this wasn't the fun, happy, and always smiling Miguel Mendoza that she knew. Yes, he got mad at her, but rarely ever raised his voice, unless he was deeply, seriously, and sincerely angry at her. But he had no reason to be right now.

"Olivia, are you listening?" Dash asked.

Olivia was jerked from her thoughts. "What?" she asked Dash, somewhat annoyed. She lay face-down on her bed. Her extremely small bedroom was barely big enough to fit her bed and desk.

"When your dad was talking to me, his eyes were blazing like fire, and he looked like he was really mad at me."

"That's weird," Olivia said, not completely paying attention.

"I also felt really cold when he was staring at me," Dash said.

There was only one reason that Olivia could think of. "I think he's going crazy," she whispered. "I feel like he's being controlled."

Suddenly, Olivia felt a vibration in her pocket. She took out her phone. There was a text from Charles telling her to hurry up. Olivia stood up and started packing her backpack. The one thing in her bedroom that Olivia was proud of was her closet. Her gigantic closet was big enough to fit four cars. But from the outside, it looked as small as an ordinary closet. She wanted to use it as her bedroom, but her dad had never seemed to believe her when she told him that it was so big. She had tried to show him the closet to prove he was wrong, but he just wouldn't come. It was always a mystery to her why he never wanted to see it, and how the closet was so big in the first place. The outside of her house didn't show it. Olivia emerged from her closet with all of the things she needed to go into the tunnel.

"How does all of that stuff fit there?" Dash asked.

Olivia felt guilty for not telling her friends about her magic closet, but it wouldn't matter to them, would it? "I just pack it well," she said and changed the topic. "We should go to your house now." Olivia grabbed her bright-purple backpack and tossed it over her shoulder. She said bye to her dad and they walked past two houses to Dash's place.

Dash's fifteen-year-old sister, Deanne, was sitting in an armchair in the living room, putting on bright-pink nail polish. The color was so bright that Olivia didn't think she could look at it for more than ten seconds.

Dash's seventeen-year-old brother Drake ran down the stairs from his room, looking for a snack. "Hey buddy!" he exclaimed, ruffling Dash's hair. "What's up?"

"Nothing," Dash said, smiling.

"Hey, Olivia," Drake said. "How's life?"

Olivia thought for a moment before responding. "Interesting," she said warily.

Drake nodded slowly and said, "See you around."

With that, he turned and walked away.

Olivia followed Dash to his bedroom upstairs and started looking for the things that Charles had written on the list. Dash grabbed a flashlight from his nightstand and the other things they needed to pack. After a few minutes, Dash's backpack was packed and he was ready to leave.

"C'mon Dash," Olivia urged. "Charles and Vivian are ready. They're waiting at the entrance of Oak Transport."

"Not so fast, Dash."

Before they could run out the door, Dash's bossy sister, Deanne, stood in front of them with her hands on her hips.

"Trying to *dash* off, aren't you?"

Dash hated it when people made fun of his name. However, Dash knew that Deanne also hated being made fun of.

"My name is cool, and I like it, *Dean,*" Dash said.

Deanne frowned at being called "Dean," and went back to applying her bright nail polish on her nails.

Dash and Olivia rushed out of the house and quickly jogged to Charles's house. They found Charles and Vivian sitting on their backpacks, playing chopsticks.

"Let's go before it gets dark," Dash said.

"It's probably going to be dark inside anyway," Olivia said.

Vivian was looking more scared now, but it was obvious she would never live it down if she didn't go in with her friends. She didn't want to miss out on the fun. And…danger?

PowerSurge took their normal formation as they headed down the stairway of the non-functioning railway station. Olivia was in the front, flanked by Dash and Charles, with Vivian right behind her. They pulled out their flashlights and Nerf guns. *Are we going to need these?* Olivia thought. *Is there anyone else here anyway?* Olivia had a tool belt strapped to her waist, so she attached the flashlight to it and held her large Nerf gun with both hands.

The kids' eyes darted around nervously for a few minutes. Then Dash threw up his hands and spoke.

"No offense to your dad, Olivia, but this is kind of boring." Dash's voice echoed throughout the open space of the train station. "I mean, I don't see anything interesting here."

Olivia nodded reluctantly.

"Maybe we should go back up," Vivian said. "Sorry, Olivia, but I never really wanted to come down here in the first place."

Olivia sighed. "Fine then. Let's go ba...." Olivia started to say.

"Hey, what's that?" Charles asked.

Charles pointed at an old caboose that had been detached from a train. It was not working anymore, but oddly, there was a small light flickering inside.

"I see a light in there," Dash said.

Vivian gripped her Nerf gun tighter than before.

"Is there someone inside?" Charles said.

"It's possible," Olivia said. "Okay, just follow what I do." She knew exactly what to do in this situation, but there was no way she would do it. She should have turned around and gone right back home, and advised her friends to do the same. But that wasn't Olivia. She wanted to know what was going on in the caboose. She aimed her Nerf gun and turned off her flashlight. The others followed her actions.

"I trust you, Olivia," Vivian said. "If anyone knows what to do, it's you."

"Yeah, Olivia knows exactly what to do," Charles said.

Olivia appreciated her friends' confidence in her. However, she only knew what to do in this situation because of her brilliantly minded dad. He could think fast in a tough situation, and he had a solution for everything. She had learned these ways by going on hikes and other scary adventures with him. She loved her dad very much, and that was why she was so concerned about him. She sent a silent prayer and then acted. She indicated that the others should turn off their flashlights too.

"Your eyes will adjust soon," Olivia whispered, as Vivian gave a little whimper.

"Vivian, stop whining," Dash complained, after Vivian whimpered again. "It's not going to help."

Vivian tilted her head, confused. "That wasn't me," she said. "It sounded like it was coming from the caboose."

Now Olivia was curious. *What was that sound then?* she wondered.

"Maybe it was an animal," Charles said. "It could have been a dog or a cat."

PowerSurge slowly crept forward, making sure that they weren't seen or heard by whatever was in the caboose. The whimper sounded again.

Olivia thought she recognized it, but she just couldn't piece together where she had heard it. However, after she looked inside the caboose, she let out a silent shriek. A flurry of words came out of her mouth as she saw her dog lying down on a table with a scared look in his eyes.

"It's Magnus!" she whispered to her friends. "What's he doing there? We have to get him out! Has he been kidnapped? Who is in there with him? What do they want from him? No!!"

"Shhhh, Olivia!" Vivian exclaimed. "We're going to get him out of there!"

"For sure!" Dash whispered.

PowerSurge moved forward, this time with Dash in the lead.

"Wait a sec," Charles whispered. "Is that Ms. B.? I mean, Agatha?" Though they were the same person, PowerSurge definitely didn't want to call her by her teacher name anymore.

It sure was. It looked exactly like her bony structure with the same long, pointy nose.

"Oh no," Vivian whispered. "What's *she* doing with him?"

Agatha seemed to be waving a pointy cane at Magnus.

"Okay, here's the plan," Charles whispered. "I'll distract her, while you guys take Magnus."

"Guys, that's what Agatha meant in her office!" Olivia whispered. "Remember? She said she was going to take something!"

Her friends exchanged glances.

"Of course!" Dash whispered. "But that other

person said the man in the household was dangerous. Was she talking about your dad?"

Olivia hadn't thought of that. *Do they know my dad?* she wondered. *How is that possible? I don't think they've ever met before. Plus, my dad would probably tell me... right?*

"Are you willing to distract her?" Vivian whispered. "You'll be in plain sight. She said she was going to kill us."

"I won't let her see me," Charles whispered. "If she does...well, that's just a risk I'm willing to take."

"Thanks, Charles," Olivia whispered. She looked at Magnus. He looked so scared. After all, he was just a puppy and had never been through something like this before. Olivia's hate for Agatha Black grew. *What does she want with my puppy?*

Agatha seemed to be mixing something inside a big pot. From where PowerSurge was positioned, Agatha wouldn't be able to see them, even if she was trying to spot them.

Charles crept behind the caboose, carefully moving every body part so as not to make a noise. Because the back of the caboose was closed, he tapped on the window with his hand and ducked below the windowsill.

Agatha came over to look through the window to

see what had made the noise. Olivia, Dash, and Vivian crept towards the side of the caboose that was open.

"Magnus, come!" Olivia whispered. She signaled with her hand. Magnus tried to run to Olivia, but he couldn't move! *Oh no! He has to come or Charles will get caught!* Olivia thought. Magnus was chained to the table. Olivia quickly dashed into the caboose, wrinkling her nose at the disgusting smell. *What is Agatha* making *in there?* Olivia thought, grossed out. She grabbed the chain that was attached to the one around Magnus's neck and tried to pull it from the ground. Her efforts were in vain. Agatha was getting closer and closer to Charles's hiding spot. Olivia frantically glanced around the caboose, looking for the key to unlock the chains. She spotted it laying on the soggy wooden floor. She grabbed it from the ground and released Magnus. Scooping him up in her arms, she ran away from the caboose and up the stairs. She escaped the underground train station and emerged into broad daylight with Magnus trailing right behind her, closely followed by Dash and Vivian.

Charles joined them a few seconds later. "I was sure we were done for," he breathed heavily. "She was about to see you guys."

"Thankfully Agatha didn't hide the key," Olivia said, trying to catch her breath. "She probably wasn't expecting anyone to come to save Magnus. She must've chained him up just so he couldn't escape. Otherwise…."

Suddenly, a piercing scream came from behind them. It was Agatha.

"You won't get away next time, you little brats!" she screeched. She was enraged. After all, whatever she had been trying to do to Magnus had failed.

PowerSurge ran down the street as fast as they could to get away from Agatha. They reached Olivia's house and slammed the door behind them, safe.

"We did it!" Vivian exclaimed. They gave each other high fives. "We beat that disgusting witch!"

Olivia wiped the sweat off her sticky forehead and sighed.

"She's angrier than ever now," Dash said. "We have to be extra careful."

"Uh…guys?" Olivia said. "Agatha must've taken Magnus after Dash and I left my house before. Magnus was here then. But so was my dad."

Charles nodded, understanding what she was trying to say.

"That means she took Magnus when your dad was home," Charles said. "Wacky."

Oliva nodded. Then she wondered. *Did my dad send us down to Oak Transport for a reason, or was it a coincidence that Magnus was there?* Not wanting her friends to think badly of her dad, Olivia didn't bring it up.

"What was Agatha even trying to do to Magnus?" Dash asked, squinting his bright eyes and wrinkling his forehead. "Hypnotize him?"

Olivia shrugged. She didn't care, as long as Magnus was safe. She reached down and patted him on his head. PowerSurge had done it again, with just another narrow escape. But would they be able to survive the next encounter with this malevolent witch?

6

"Hi Dad," Olivia greeted cheerfully. Her friends were relaxing at her house after the thrilling experience they had had at Oak Transport. They were sitting in the small living room, which only contained a petite, tiled coffee table, two couches, and a small television. However, Olivia was very proud of the shelves lining the walls that were filled with books, from classic novels to fantasy, and science-fiction. The coffee table was a beautiful, white color and always sparkled in the sunlight. Many windows were spread out across the living room walls, filling the room with natural light. The coffee table was barely big enough for Olivia and her dad to play board games, although they still did that a lot. The couches were made of black leather and always stayed cool in the summer. Her television worked, but it was ancient. It had been her grandpa's—that's why it was so old. She could still watch shows, but they were all in black and white. She didn't use it much because she also had a phone. She and her dad had scraped together just enough money to buy two—one for her and one for him. They needed to communicate as Olivia's dad was a working parent and had to raise Olivia by himself. Olivia loved the look that the bookshelves brought to the room. They gave it a classical look as well as made the inhabitants look well educated. The shelves were black wood, and the spectrum of the colors on the books almost invited Olivia to come read them. Olivia didn't care that her house was small because it had history, and it had character. That was what she loved about it.

"Hi." Olivia's dad yawned, stretching his arms. He had just woken up from a long nap, spanning the whole time PowerSurge was in Oak Transport. "How was your adventure?"

PowerSurge looked at each other. They were all thinking the same thing. Was it safe to tell anyone about their discovery? Who could they trust? Clearly, Dash thought telling Olivia's dad was okay. He told Olivia's dad all about what happened at school and in

Oak Transport. Charles, Vivian, and Olivia jumped in to correct something when necessary. Dash wasn't an excellent storyteller. He included unnecessary details such as 'Oak Transport used to serve some delicious potato chips' and 'he really likes tomatoes, by the way.'

When Dash finished telling the story, Olivia's dad looked completely amazed. "You kids did all of that without any help?" he asked. "That's amazing!"

Olivia turned red. *Dad is awesome,* she thought. *I know he won't tell a single soul about any of this.*

"But be careful," he added grimly. "You don't know what you're up against. Others can be extremely harmful, and you need to know that before you go on missions like these."

"Thanks, Dad," Olivia said. She had no idea why she had ever doubted him. All of a sudden, she felt really tired. After all, so much had happened in one day. "I'm going to sleep early today." She yawned.

Dash looked surprised. "What about dinner?" he asked, looking at her like she had just committed a crime.

Olivia shook her head. *Oh, I completely forgot about dinner!* Olivia thought. Dash never skipped a meal. He loved food, almost as much as he loved basketball.

"I'll help you make a sandwich," Vivian said.

Olivia and Vivian stood up and went into the

cramped kitchen. Except for a few cabinets, a little refrigerator, and an island in the center, the kitchen was empty. The wooden cabinets weren't painted. Olivia didn't like that; she always wanted to paint them a beautiful, glossy white. They were not very sturdy. Olivia and her dad had to be careful of the weight the cabinets were holding, as they weren't strongly bolted to the wall. Thankfully, they didn't own many utensils or silverware. The Mendozas lived a very simple life, though they had enough to keep them going, which was all that mattered. They used a drink refrigerator for their fridge, as they didn't have enough money to buy a big one. It was crammed with leftover food and groceries, and they could barely close the door without it popping open again. Olivia's kitchen island was the only item in her kitchen she was proud of. It was beautiful, sturdily built of white wood, almost as big as the kitchen itself. A beautiful white marble countertop was glazed over the top, adding a lively touch to the kitchen. It was built by Olivia's grandpa, and he and his wife had maintained it every day to look impeccably spotless. Olivia's grandpa was the nicest person she had ever known. He was so kind, sweet, and gentle to her. They would often stay up late reading stories together. Olivia was devastated when he mysteriously died. Nobody could figure out how he had died; not even high-class detectives and scientists. There was not a single clue on his body. Living in limited space made her realize that she really didn't need much. Charles's house was huge, but it was so full of things he didn't really need.

Olivia opened the mini-fridge and grabbed some ham, cheese, and bread. "Do you want one too?" she asked Vivian, as she buttered the bread.

"Okay," Vivian said. "But I'll make a PB&J sandwich." She was a vegetarian, but she was okay with watching other people eat meat.

I wish I could be a vegetarian, Olivia thought. *It's just that meat gives me lots of protein, and I could never have the willpower not to eat it.* Vivian just wouldn't eat it herself because she had a huge soft spot for animals.

"Sure." Olivia opened one of the cabinets and took out some peanut butter and jelly.

At the smell of food being made, Magnus appeared right next to her. He looked up at her with his beautiful blue eyes, and his bright pink tongue was hanging out of his mouth. Olivia knew she shouldn't, but she gave him a bread crust.

"Here, Magnus," she said, as she tore off a piece of bread and handed it to him. It was gone before she could blink.

Olivia's dad strolled into the room. "Are you

feeding him off the counter again?" he asked.

"Yeah, sorry, Dad," she said. "He's just so cute. Plus, he's been through so much today. Who knows what would've happened to him if we hadn't gotten to Oak Transport when we did?"

"I know, but you can't give into him," her dad said. He walked over to the other side of the table, and took a seat in one of the two chairs. Magnus appeared at his side. Olivia's dad reached down and patted him on his head.

Olivia finished making her sandwich. Suddenly, she realized that she wasn't really hungry.

"Here, Dad," she said, as she placed it in front of him. "You can have this."

"You don't want it?" he asked.

Olivia shook her head.

He started eating, putting a clean napkin on his lap. "Thanks, Olivia," he mumbled as he took a bite out of it.

Vivian sat down across from him with her sandwich. She started eating.

Olivia left them to it and went to see what Dash and Charles were up to. They were busily whispering to each other in the living room.

"Hey, guys," she said, as she sat down next to Dash on the big couch. "What are you talking about?"

"Charles just brought up a good point," Dash said. "What if Agatha is part of a gang of witches?"

Olivia wondered why she hadn't considered this before. "Of course!" she exclaimed. "That would explain who she was talking to when we were hiding in her office." Olivia shuddered at the thought of that experience.

"Maybe it was the leader of her gang," Charles said, as he twiddled his thumbs. He also seemed nervous about facing Agatha again. "And all of the pictures hanging on the office walls might've been the other witches in the gang!"

"Vivian!" Dash called. "Come here!"

Vivian appeared in the doorway, chewing her sandwich. She sat next to Olivia and looked questioningly at Dash. "What's up?"

Charles shifted his position. "We think Agatha might be part of a gang of witches," he said. "It would make more sense."

Vivian nodded, a little pale from the thought. "Definitely a possibility," she said. "Thanks for telling me, but I'm going to get back to my sandwich now." She stood up and walked out of the room to the kitchen.

We never keep secrets from each other, Olivia thought proudly. *I think that's probably why we're such great friends!*

"Well." Olivia yawned as she stood up. "I'm going to bed. See you guys at school tomorrow."

Olivia said bye to her friends who were about to go home and walked down the hallway. She stopped halfway. "Oh, and Dad?" she added, turning around. "Can you write me an excuse note? No time to do homework today!"

7

Olivia crawled into her small bed. Its size just about allowed her to lie down with a few inches to spare. *I just want to sleep now,* she thought. She was so tired that she fell asleep before her head hit the pillow—literally. However, after what felt like seconds later, her eyes opened. A man was seated in front of her on a wooden chair. He seemed to be in a never-ending canvas of white. She squinted at him. *It can't be!* she thought. *But he looks exactly like him!*

"Grandpa?" she asked disbelievingly. "What are you doing here?"

Olivia missed her grandpa so much. He had been her role model. She was absolutely devastated when he died. She had only been in kindergarten, but they had been so close. It remained a mystery how he died. He was perfectly healthy one night, but the next morning, he just didn't wake up. The police hadn't been able to figure out how he passed away. They spent hours each day trying to solve the mystery—ending up unsuccessful. The one thing that they found was a small green mark on the back of his neck, like nothing anyone had seen before. He was her dad's father. Olivia and her dad both inherited a lot of traits from him. His bright brown eyes and light brown hair were identical to those of Olivia's dad. But her grandpa had something that was completely unique. Nobody else had the soft expression in his eyes. It always comforted Olivia when she was feeling upset or hurt, and instantly made her feel better.

"My little girl," he whispered. His eyes were sparkling just the way Olivia always remembered. "I have an important message for you."

"What, Abuelo?" Olivia asked, referring to her grandpa in Spanish. *Was her grandpa really here in order to convey an important message to her? I must be dreaming!* Olivia thought. *He's not alive anymore. And I'm no prophet! I must be remembering him in a dream.*

"Listen to me," he answered. "I am very proud of you for everything you have done, but I want you to be careful. Agatha Black is not someone to mess with."

"Why?" Olivia asked. *The witches?* she thought. *Has Grandpa come to tell me important information about the witches?* She was eager to know what he was going to tell her.

"That is not important," her grandpa said. "Right now I need to tell you what to do." He waited until Olivia's bright brown eyes were locked on his. "Your father was good friends with three kids when he was younger. They happened to be the parents of the children of PowerSurge—the parents who are not alive. They called themselves the Blazing Stars, and they tried to defeat Agatha and her gang of witches."

"Really?" asked Olivia. *Why didn't my dad ever tell me this?* she thought. "What happened?"

"What do you mean?" her grandpa asked.

Olivia looked at him. "You said they *tried?"* she said. "What is that supposed to mean? They failed or something?"

Her grandpa smiled. "Yes," he said. "They did. They tried very hard, but Agatha's gang of witches was too good for them. Listen to me. Agatha is part of a gang of witches called the Black Death. Their leader is VERY powerful, and you must stay away from her. Her name is Agnes Howler, and I don't want you to ever go looking for her. She will kill you and your friends if she needs to. And she definitely won't let anything get in her way. You must defeat these witches."

"Why me?" Olivia asked.

"Because I know you are the only person who can do it," her grandpa said. "And because I believe in you. Now, you remember Max, right?"

Olivia nodded eagerly. "Of course!" she cried.

"Good," her grandpa said. "Four years ago, the Black Death captured him. They also captured someone else before you were born—your brother."

"My brother?" Olivia gasped. "But…I…I don't…."

"Yes, you do," her grandpa interrupted with a smile. "He's older than you. You weren't born when he was taken. But now is not the time to talk about that. You can save him. Listen to me very carefully. At five minutes before midnight, go to the edge of Lockhart Woods, right beside your house. Follow the voice calling for you. You will reach a moonlit lake. When the watch informs you that it is the stroke of midnight, you need to jump into the lake. You must find the magic compass in order to locate the missing children. Once you have done that, you must find something called the Mystic Pearl. It is the key to the defeat of the witches, but also the key to their success. You have one week, or all hope will be lost."

"You mean I have to do all this in one week!" she

exclaimed, tripping over her words. "Which watch do we use to find the witch? What will happen when we jump in? How do we know it's the right lake? What do you mean by 'follow the voice'? What is the Mystic Pearl? *What?*"

Her grandpa merely smiled and shook his head. "Save the questions," he said.

How can I save them? Olivia thought. *I need to know in order to succeed.*

"You'll figure it out as you go." Her grandpa pulled something out of the pocket of his ragged jeans, the ones he always wore. It was a silver necklace with a purple gem set in its pendant. "Olivia, if you ever need guidance from me, rub this gem with your hands. But remember, you can only use it once." He handed the necklace to her. "I have to go now, but remember, I will always be watching you, my girl. I love you!"

Olivia treasured his smile one last time before it was time to return to the real world. "Bye!" she whispered.

She placed the necklace over her head. With that, her grandpa faded away, and she woke with a start.

8

Olivia rubbed her eyes, feeling like she hadn't even gotten a minute of sleep. Her first thoughts were that her dream wasn't real, but when she felt the purple gem pressing against her chest, she knew it had truly happened. She reluctantly got out of bed and threw on a white T-shirt and jeans, and quickly gobbled down some cereal. Her dad was still asleep when she left for school, and she didn't want to disturb him. He was muttering something like "She has found you." But Olivia left anyway, even though she was quite curious about what she had heard her father say in his sleep.

Olivia cycled to school, pedaling as fast as she could. When she saw Vivian, Charles, and Dash waiting for her in the school's front yard with faces both excited and sad, she hurried over to them. "Guys, guys, you won't believe what I dreamt about last night!"

They listened to her story with wide eyes. But she left out the part about the hope of finding Max and her own brother. *I'd better keep that to myself, for now,* Olivia thought. *I don't want them to set their hopes too high, in case we don't succeed.*

"No way!" Charles exclaimed.

"Guess what!" Dash almost yelled. "We each had a dream too. My mom gave me a shrunken eagle cart. When we need to get somewhere, I can just enlarge it and the eagles take us there!"

"And I got a magic watch!" Charles exclaimed. He pulled up his sleeve to show it to Olivia. "My dad said you would know how to use it. But he did tell me that it could get us out of a certain place. Something like that."

"And my dad gave me a flashlight!" Vivian said. "It can see things that are invisible. And he told me that the witches fly to their meetings on canes that make them invisible!"

So they have magical items, not just magical powers! Olivia thought. *That's cool, but it makes it even harder for us to prevail!*

"But the magical devices can only be used once,

except for the flashlight," Charles said.

"I wonder why that is," Olivia said. "Why the flashlight specifically? Maybe we'll need to use it many times."

"Yeah. Why were we given these devices?" Dash asked. "Will they really work? And why do *we* have to defeat the Black Death? We're just kids."

"No idea," Vivian said, shaking her head. "Maybe we're the only ones who can?"

Olivia felt pressured, as if the world depended on them being able to succeed. "Now we're onto something!" Olivia exclaimed.

The warning bell rang. "See you guys in a little bit!" Olivia said.

The day went by. PowerSurge was so excited about their discoveries—until they were on their way to science class. PowerSurge was walking down the Hallway of Terror. Olivia shrank away from the dirtiest parts of the hallway, trying not to throw up. Kids had spilled weird liquids and food all over the floor. The Walter Bryce Academy janitor was very old. It seemed like she had given up on trying to clean the Hallway of Terror; therefore kids occasionally found pieces of chewing gum stuck to their shoes.

"I wish each of your parents and my grandpa were still alive," Olivia said. "The dream really really made me miss my grandpa. Plus, if they were here, they would be able to give us guidance whenever we wanted it."

"Yeah," Dash said. "I feel sad too. But we need to stay positive if we're going to defeat these witches."

Charles nodded in agreement.

"I'm nervous," Vivian said. "What if Aga…, sorry, I mean Ms. B. doesn't treat us normally? Or maybe she won't even let us into the classroom!"

After Vivian corrected herself from saying Ms. B.'s real name, Olivia thought, *Good job Vivian. We're at school and we can't risk anyone hearing about our discovery.*

"She sort of has to," Olivia said. She dropped her pencil case. Dash bent down to pick it up. "If she doesn't, she knows we will reveal her secret."

"Olivia," Charles complained, after she dropped her galaxy decorated science binder. "If you carry stuff on your head like that, you're going to drop everything!"

Olivia always carried her supplies on her head for some reason. It freed up one hand because she only needed one to steady her supplies from time to time. "I'm not dropping anything," she said. Then, to contradict her words, her matching galaxy science notebook fell off her head.

Charles grinned at her.

"Oh, fine." Olivia frowned as she used both hands to steady her things.

PowerSurge was standing outside of the door to the science classroom.

"What are you waiting for, jerks?" asked Hawk as he shouldered them aside and pushed the door open.

Arsen shoved PowerSurge into the classroom, and Vivian fell over.

"What was that for?" asked Olivia, as she helped Vivian up. *Do those guys have nothing better to do with their time besides push people?* Olivia wondered, annoyed.

"No clue," Dash said.

PowerSurge took their seats; this time, towards the back of the classroom.

When Ms. B. turned around, her eyes followed their every movement. "Hello, class," she greeted them in her piercing cold voice. "Please take out your homework."

Olivia opened her science binder. She knew that Ms. B. would try to find an excuse to cause trouble. If Olivia didn't have her homework completed, it would be a golden opportunity for Ms. B. to punish Olivia. To avoid that crisis, Olivia had done it during lunch. Ms. B. glared angrily in Olivia's direction after she saw that Olivia had completed her homework. Olivia felt satisfied. *What?* she thought, feeling mischievous. *It's not my fault that we know your secret!*

"Now, who would like to answer the first problem?" Ms. B. asked. "How about you, Jordan?"

The student who she had picked on, Jordan, was not very smart. There was only one level of science class available for all fifth graders. Science class was easy for most of the kids. To answer the first question, all that was needed was to name two elements on the periodic table.

"How about taco and burrito?" Jordan said. He wasn't trying to make the class laugh, he sincerely thought that was the answer. Everyone in the class started laughing except for Ms. B.

"Principal's office, Sanders," Ms. B. said casually.

Jordan stood up and walked sulkily to the door.

"Quickly!" Ms. B. said sharply. Turning to the classroom, she added, "Anyone who doesn't want to learn is welcome to leave."

Everybody stayed glued to their seats out of fear. But Olivia was focused on something else. She smelled something that was worse than rotten eggs and spoiled milk mixed together. *Yuck! What is that smell!* Olivia thought, holding her nose and looking around. She spotted a bland, green-colored drink sitting on Ms. B.'s desk. To Olivia's horror, Ms. B. walked over to it and *drank* it. *Yuck!* Olivia shuddered.

"Vivian, first question please," said Ms. B., as if nothing had happened.

"Oxygen and Hydrogen," said Vivian.

Ms. B. looked thoughtful for a second. "Too simple," she scolded. "Detention."

"What!" Olivia burst out loud. "That's so unfair! Vivian didn't even do anything wrong, Ag...." She was silenced by a sudden yell from Ms. B.

"You too!" Ms. B. shouted before Olivia could say her real name. "And you!" she shouted, pointing at Dash and Charles. "Leave the room now!"

Charles and Dash shrugged their shoulders and walked out of the room with Olivia and Vivian.

The rest of the class was confused. They could tell there had to be more to this than just Vivian giving too simple of an answer.

PowerSurge left the classroom and walked down the hallway. "What are we going to do now?" Olivia asked. She only had one class left: history. She usually enjoyed history, however, she didn't think she would today.

"I guess we'll just have to sneak out of detention," Dash said, as he took his music sheets out of his locker. He and Vivian had music, but Charles and Olivia had history last period on Tuesday.

I still don't get why we got detention! Olivia thought.

I've never gotten detention before! This is so ....UGH!

"How are the three of us supposed to tell our parents we got detention?" Vivian said. "We can't tell them about the Black Death! At least Olivia's dad knows. Maybe he can cover for us?"

Olivia nodded.

"It sucks that Ms. B. still has power over us because she's our teacher," Dash said. "I wish she wasn't able to give us detention or anything!"

"How are we going to sneak out of detention?" asked Charles, as he banged his locker closed. "The rule is whichever teacher gives you detention gets to watch you. Agatha is pretty much going to be staring at us the whole time."

"We'll find a way," Vivian said. "I know we will."

At these words, PowerSurge separated. Olivia's history teacher, Ms. Anderson, was very nice. She gladly excused Olivia and Charles from their homework assignments. They promised to have them completed by the end of the week. Ms. Anderson's history lectures were really interesting, but today, Olivia had no clue what was going on. She was buried deep in her disturbed thoughts. When the final bell of the day rang, she was off to detention.

"Where are we supposed to go?" Olivia asked Charles. She wasn't used to being in trouble, so she had no clue what she was supposed to do.

"We should probably just go to the science classroom," Charles said.

Since the school day was over, he and Olivia walked to their lockers to gather their things. Olivia stuffed her binders, notebooks, textbooks, and other things into her backpack. It was really heavy because she was carrying four binders, five notebooks, and three textbooks. She hung her backpack over her shoulder and waited for Charles to finish packing up his things.

Dash and Vivian arrived at their lockers.

"Hey, guys," greeted Dash. "I have good news. Mrs. Brody excused me from my detention. She said as long as I've learned my lesson, it's okay. Oh, and, Ms. B. said to meet her in the science classroom."

"Yaaay," Olivia said sarcastically. Lowering her voice, she added, "I think I know a way to sneak out."

Her friends looked excited at the mention of this.

"How?" Charles asked, zipping up his backpack. It was so heavy that he had to use two arms to pick it up.

"There's a door connecting the middle school science classroom to ours," Olivia said. "We'll take the seats next to it. One of us can go up to her and ask her a question about the homework. Then the others can sneak out."

"That's good," Charles said. "But what about the

other person? How are they going to get out?"

"I'll be that person," Olivia answered. "I'm sure I can find some way out."

"I have an idea!" Vivian exclaimed as she slammed her locker door shut. "How about the other three who are already out make a noise to distract her, so Ms. B. gets up and goes outside?"

"Then the person who is still left can sneak out!" Dash finished for her.

"Exactly," Charles said. "Let's do this!"

PowerSurge headed to the science room. *Is it going to work?* Olivia thought as they walked down the Hallway of Terror for the umpteenth time that day. *I really hope it does!* She would be the one asking Ms. B. the question.

Walking into the room, PowerSurge started towards the unoccupied seats beside the door that led to the middle school science room.

But Ms. B. had other plans for them. "Where do you think you're going?" she asked, pointing at them with a long, bony finger.

Charles glared at her, desperately trying to hide his annoyance. "To those unoccupied seats right there," he said calmly, gesturing towards the chairs they were planning to take.

Ms. B. shook her head. "I want you guys right

here," she said sinisterly. She walked over to the four seats that were right in front of her desk.

Oh no! Olivia thought worriedly. *How in the world are Dash, Vivian, and Charles going to get out without being seen now?*

PowerSurge reluctantly made their way to the chairs and took their seats. Eyeing the door to the middle school science room, Olivia felt her hope of escaping slowly start to drain.

Five minutes after everyone was seated, Olivia realized that there was no time to waste. She stood up, with a piece of paper containing the science homework in her hand. There were other kids in detention, so it wouldn't be too obvious when Vivian, Charles, and Dash snuck out, but Ms. B. would be sure to notice. She would probably be expecting something like this to happen. Olivia walked up to Ms. B.'s desk. She tried to position herself so that her body would obstruct Ms. B.'s view of Dash, Vivian, and Charles.

"Excuse me, Miss," she whispered. "I need help with problem four of the homework."

Ms. B. sat up straight. "Figure it out yourself," she growled. "It is called homework for a reason. It is not to be done at school with a teacher's help."

She was about to turn back to the class. Olivia saw that Dash, Vivian, and Charles were out of their seats and were crawling on the ground. If Ms. B. turned around now, she would notice them, and certainly send them back to their seats.

"Wait, but can I at least have a hint?" Olivia asked. She was desperately trying to distract Ms. B. Her friends needed just a little more time to escape successfully. They were now at the door, trying to open it slowly without making any noise.

"Of course you can't have a hint," Ms. B. said rudely. "Now go back to your seat, and next time, pay attention in class."

I don't understand how Ms. B. qualifies as nice enough to be a teacher at our school, Olivia thought. *She's not fair to the children. At all.* However, Olivia smiled inside as Ms. B. gave her an annoyed glare. Dash, Vivian, and Charles had silently slipped out the door, and they were safe from their unnecessary detention. Now Olivia had to wait for the loud noise outside so she could sneak out of the door unnoticed. She sat down in her chair again, after completing phase one of the escape.

Ms. B. turned around. At first, she didn't notice that Olivia's friends were gone, but when her eyes reached the empty desks where they had been sitting, she suddenly turned on Olivia. "You," she growled.

Olivia could see that her eyes were completely red now and her necklace was really bright. It was really creeping Olivia out to look at them, but she didn't say anything.

"Stay for an extra hour! Now go back to your seat!"

Confused, Olivia didn't think Ms. B. realized she was already sitting in her seat. Suddenly, Olivia heard a loud clanging sound outside.

Ms. B. stood up to go investigate. She glanced at Olivia. "DO NOT MOVE A MUSCLE!" she shouted.

Wow, I'm surprised she's actually falling for it. Olivia thought. *I don't even feel bad for tricking a teacher because it's Ms. B.'s fault we're here! We shouldn't be in detention in the first place!*

Ms. B.'s face came so close that Olivia could smell her stinky breath emanating from her yellow and rotten teeth.

"I'm serious," she warned Olivia with an extremely stern voice.

After Ms. B. went outside to check out what was happening, Olivia quickly grabbed her backpack and snuck out the door adjoining the two science classrooms. Luckily, there were not many other kids in the room, so they wouldn't tell on Olivia. *Please don't snitch!* Olivia thought. *Oh well, it doesn't matter because Ms. B. will know I escaped anyway.* Olivia was safely in the other identical room now. She waited until she heard Ms. B.'s enraged yell from the other room until she knew it was safe to leave the next classroom. When she saw her friends outside, she gave them a high-five.

"That was great guys!" she exclaimed. "What did you do?" A toppled over shelf behind Charles answered her question.

"Yeah," Vivian said. "I feel bad for pushing a shelf, but it worked."

"Oh, don't feel bad," Charles said. "She was pretty obviously just giving us detention because she wanted to be flat-out mean."

"We should go before Ms. B. comes out again," Dash said.

"Good idea," Olivia said.

PowerSurge dashed towards the main exit of the school and ran outside. The school video cameras had probably caught them sneaking out of detention, but it was definitely worth the risk.

"How are we supposed to get to your house, Olivia?" Vivian asked. "Olivia's the only one with a bike! The rest of us take the bus or get driven here in the morning."

"That's true!" Olivia exclaimed. "How are we supposed to get home? It's too late for the bus and the next school bus comes in an hour!"

"Maybe we can all just sit on the bicycle?" Charles said. "We could take turns pedaling."

Dash shook his head. "That wouldn't be much faster than walking," he said. "We could call one of our parents to pick us up?"

"No, they'd ask what we're doing at school so late," Vivian said. "They probably assume that we're at somebody else's house right now, so if we told them to pick us up at school, they'd be suspicious."

Hearing a familiar chant, Olivia thought of an idea. "Hey guys, there's an eighth-grade football game today!" Olivia exclaimed, pointing at the cheerleaders who were walking down the sidewalk. "Don't they always go on a school bus?"

"Yeah, we could probably hop on!" Dash exclaimed. "But what if they go the opposite direction of your house, Olivia?"

"I guess it's just a risk we have to take," Vivian said. "The bigger question is, how are we going to get on the bus? I doubt they would let us just hop on."

"Follow my lead," Olivia said, getting an idea.

In a minute, the bus pulled up to the curb, and boys in football uniforms got on, followed by some cheerleaders. Olivia gestured to her friends to follow her onto the bus.

"Excuse me, you can't get on," Coach Frenzick said before they could hop on.

Olivia was ready to reply. "We're part of the

yearbook committee. We're here to take pictures of the football team."

Coach Frenzick frowned. "Why didn't Mr. Haynes inform me about this?" he asked. "He's the supervisor of the yearbook committee."

"I'm not sure," Olivia said. "It probably slipped his mind. We're just going to take pictures on our phones. That's all. We promise."

Coach Frenzick nodded. "Alright, but next time tell Mr. Haynes to inform me."

PowerSurge got on the bus.

"Well, that was smart," Vivian said, taking one of the seats inside the bus.

"Yeah, I definitely wouldn't have thought of that one," Charles said.

"Agreed, great idea, Olivia," Dash said.

Olivia smiled. "Thanks, guys," she said. "Now we just have to hope that they go the direction of my house." As soon as she sat down next to Vivian and put her backpack on the ground, the bus took off—in the right direction!

"YES YES YES YES YES YES YES!" Vivian exclaimed, jumping in her seat.

Some cheerleaders nearby looked at her, confused.

"Sorry, it's my first time taking pictures for the committee," Vivian said, quickly covering it up.

"Guys, how are we going to get off the bus at the right place?" Charles asked, leaning over the aisle from his seat beside Dash. "We definitely don't want to go all the way north to Carrington. That's about a four-hour walk from Olivia's house." His voice was almost drowned out by the loud shouting of the boys on the football team.

"I have an okay idea, but I think it's our best bet," Dash said.

PowerSurge rode on for a few minutes, not saying anything to one another.

"Okay, we're getting close to my house now," Olivia said. "What's your idea, Dash?"

Dash stood up and walked to the front of the bus, steadying himself by putting his hands on the benches. He reached the front.

"Uh, sir?" Dash stopped in front of Coach Frenzick. "There was a misunderstanding. Mr. Haynes accidentally assigned two groups to the football game. He doesn't need us to go. If you could just stop right here, we could get off."

Coach Frenzick looked confused. "Yes sure, but are you sure you want us to drop you off here? After we drop the boys off, the bus driver can take you back to the school," he said.

Dash wobbled on his legs. "No, no, that's okay.

Um, my aunt lives here. We'll go to her house," Dash said quickly.

Coach Frenzick nodded slowly and told the bus driver to stop the bus.

PowerSurge got hopped off the bus a block away from Olivia's house.

"Another great idea award goes to Dash!" Charles exclaimed. "We're here!"

"Wow, great teamwork guys!" Vivian congratulated Olivia and Dash and threw her backpack over her shoulders.

"Thanks," Olivia said. "Come on, let's go inside."

"What time should we leave?" Vivian asked, as they walked down the block.

"My grandpa said we need to be at the lake five minutes before midnight," Olivia said. "So probably around 11:45 PM. But how are you guys going to even sneak out?"

Her friends looked at each other. This was the first time they had considered that.

"I'm not sure. Maybe through our bedroom windows?" Dash said.

Vivian shook her head. "That's not safe though," she said. "We'll just have to take our chances with the front door."

Charles nodded in agreement.

"We'll come back to Olivia's house at 11:30," Dash said. "Olivia, meet us in your kitchen."

Olivia nodded. Her friends knew the passcode to her front door. At least her house had a keypad on the front door to enter. The house wasn't very advanced, but it had a satisfactory safety system.

"Good thing our houses are close enough for us to be able to bike there," Vivian said. "Otherwise, we would have a problem."

Everyone nodded in agreement.

"Will meeting at 11:30 give us enough time to get to the lake though?" asked Charles. "We don't know how far the voice will lead us or how deep in the woods the lake will be."

"Olivia's grandpa said five minutes before midnight exactly," Dash said. "Maybe if we leave before or after that exact time, it won't work."

What would happen if we jumped in the lake without doing the right things before? Olivia thought.

"You know, we don't even know what will happen if we jump in the lake," Olivia said thoughtfully. "Where do you think it will take us?"

"There's only one way to find out." Vivian grinned.

After Olivia entered her house and put her backpack in her room, she knew something was missing. "Where's my dad?" she asked, looking around the house.

"Maybe he's sleeping in his room," said Charles. He checked in Olivia's dad's room. "Nope, not there."

Suddenly, the front door opened. Olivia's dad came in, panting. His hazel-brown hair, that was almost always clean, was covered with leaves. His face and clothes were covered in dirt. His body had many scratches and cuts.

"Dad, what happened?" Olivia said. She ran to his side and started brushing him off. *Where did you go?* she thought. *What were you doing?*

"Nothing," he said. "Just went for a little…um…uh…stroll in the woods." He was acting like nothing had happened.

Olivia was extremely concerned now. She looked at her friends with a scared look on her face.

Vivian looked scared too, while Charles and Dash looked more worried.

Something was definitely wrong with Olivia's dad, and they needed to get to the bottom of it.

9

It was a cloudy Wednesday morning and Olivia was lying on her back on her bed. She stared up at her imaginary planets and stars on the ceiling of her small room. She had about ten minutes before she had to leave for school, and she was feeling extremely lonely. She eyed the necklace resting on her chest. She knew that if she wanted to use the necklace to talk to her grandpa, she would have to ask permission from the rest of her friends. She was missing her grandpa a lot because she had just seen him in her dreams. She stood up and walked across her room. There was a beautiful wooden cabinet with a dark brown tint attached to the wall, at about her height. She opened it and took a deep breath. This cabinet had been her grandpa's, and she thought that it still smelled like him.

"I miss you, Grandpa," she whispered, as she rested her head against the cabinet door. She quickly closed the door, so the aura of her grandpa wouldn't escape the cabinet.

Suddenly, she realized that she and her friends had completely forgotten about the visit they were supposed to make to the woods last night! She took her phone out of her pocket and dialed Dash's number.

He answered in a few seconds. "What's up, Olivia?"

Olivia spoke into the phone. "We forgot about going to the woods last night!"

"We didn't forget," he said. "We came to get you at your house at 11:30. Your dad told us to leave."

"What!" Olivia gasped. "That literally makes no sense! It's not something my dad would do. Although it's not like you guys come to my house at 11:30 every day, but still! He didn't ask you why you were here?"

"No, he just told us to go. I'm really not sure why he would do that," Dash said. "I thought you maybe told him to not let us come in because you weren't ready or something."

"Nope, I definitely didn't tell him anything," she said. "Anyway, did you guys go anyway? How was it?"

"How could we go without you?" Dash asked. "No way."

Olivia smiled. She was glad she had such great friends she could always count on. "Let's try again tonight," she said into the phone. "I hope you guys can sneak out of your houses again."

"Me too," said Dash. "By the way, you should probably get going before you get to school late."

"Wait, how do you know where I am?" Olivia asked. *Is Dash watching me?* Olivia thought. She looked around her room.

"Let's just say I know you better than you think," Dash laughed. "But seriously, get a move on."

"Thanks, Dash," Olivia said. "See you at school."

"Bye!" Dash hung up.

Olivia slung her backpack over one of her shoulders. She checked her watch and ran out of the room. She had fifteen minutes to get to school, which started at 8:30 AM. Her bike ride would cut the time close. She quickly chugged a glass of milk and said bye to her dad.

While Olivia was biking to school, she suddenly realized something that almost made her fall off her bicycle. She had science for the first period! *Oh no! Ms. B. is going to kill me if I'm late!* Olivia thought. *Literally!* Olivia peddled faster knowing that Ms. B. would eagerly look for any possible way to get PowerSurge in trouble after what had happened at Oak Transport. Plus, they had escaped detention! Would Ms. B. get angry at them in front of the whole class? Olivia didn't think so. That would be so embarrassing to Ms. B.! After all, what kind of teacher lets kids escape from detention?

Walter Bryce Elementary School soon came into her view. The building was brown, but still appealing to those who passed by. The windows were glowing in the bright sunlight, catching the reflective rays of the blazing sun. Olivia quickly parked her bike in the bicycle rack in front of the school. She flung the black door open and ran inside the school. *It's against school policy to run!* her cautious side warned. *Oh, forget it!* her logical side countered.

Olivia dashed down one of the school's good hallways and ran past her locker, which was near the math classroom. Olivia didn't even bother to put her backpack in her locker. She ran to the science classroom, knowing that her science binder and homework were already in her backpack.

Ms. B. was doing the morning attendance. "Olivia Mendoza?" Ms. B. called.

Olivia was just on time. She ran inside the room, her backpack still hanging on her back. "Here!" panted

Olivia, sliding into her seat.

Ms. B. gave her a silent but meaningful stare, warning her that she had just missed getting in trouble.

Olivia was lucky that her name wasn't Anthony Alengate; he was always called first in attendance. *Phew, that was close!* Olivia thought.

Charles grinned at her from his seat by the window.

"Good," Ms. B. growled. She finished the morning attendance and dove right into the boring lesson, which was a lecture.

"Excuse me," Robin Panthers said. "You forgot to stamp our homework!"

The rest of the class nodded in agreement.

"Alright then," sighed Ms. B. She quickly walked to her desk and took the stamp off of its ink pad. She walked towards the back row of the classroom, where Olivia was sitting. However, after Olivia locked eyes with her, she suddenly jerked to a stop and started with the first row instead. Ms. B. slowly made her way to the back of the classroom, stamping everyone's homework.

To Olivia's surprise, when it was finally her turn to be stamped, Ms. B. skipped her, as if pretending she wasn't there. "Miss, you skipped me," Olivia said.

Ms. B. threw up her hands. "Why is it that you children care so much about these silly stamps?" she exclaimed. She walked back to her desk and put down the stamp.

Olivia thought that Ms. B had purposely avoided stamping her paper.

"As I was saying before I was so rudely interrupted." Ms. B. glared at Robin. "Who can name the atomic number for gold?"

Charles's hand shot up faster than Olivia could process the question or even blink.

"Anyone?" Ms. B.'s eyes scanned the room, purposely ignoring Charles.

Why is she so mean to Charles? Olivia thought. *Is it because he's smarter than her?*

"Umm, hello?" Charles said bravely.

Ms. B. rolled her eyes and threw back her head, extremely annoyed. "Fine, go on, Williams," Ms. B. sighed. "But you other kids better know the answer as well. These types of questions will come up on the test tomorrow."

"It's 79," Charles said.

Olivia wasn't listening. She stared out the window at a black shape moving along the sidewalk. *What is that?* she wondered. *Is it a person?* Olivia peeked at Ms. B. *Is she smiling?* Olivia was sure Ms. B. was looking out the window too. Olivia focused on the hooded figure. The shape was definitely a human. As the shape turned to face the window, Olivia was ready. She snapped a picture with her phone and hid it back under her desk.

"Miss Mendoza," Ms. B. suddenly appeared behind Olivia and held out one hand. Her other arm was crossed over her chest, and her icy eyes were cold, without the respect or sympathy in them that a teacher should have. "Phone, please."

Come on! Olivia thought. *Wait a sec, is she taking my phone because she* saw *me take the picture? Is there a connection between Ms. B. and the person on the front lawn?* Olivia shook her head. *No, of course not! I can't make assumptions! How would I know?*

Olivia quickly changed her phone screen to a text exchange she had shared with her partner for her English project so Ms. B. wouldn't see the picture. Olivia turned her phone off so that Ms. B. would need a passcode to log on. Olivia reluctantly placed her phone on the skinny palm of Ms. B.'s bony hand.

"Get it from me after class."

Dash raised an eyebrow at her.

Olivia motioned that she would tell him about it later when Ms. B. wasn't listening.

After science, PowerSurge had a five-minute break before their next class. They were standing by their lockers when Olivia remembered she had forgotten to pick up her phone from Ms. B. after class.

"Guys, I have to get my phone from Ms. B. I need it to show you something," Olivia said. *I wouldn't have to if that annoying woman kept her nose in her own, disgusting business!* she thought.

Olivia slammed her locker door shut and locked it. She started down the Hallway of Terror toward the science wing. Walter Bryce Academy was a K-12 school, so it accommodated students who were from age five to seventeen. Unfortunately for every student, all of the classrooms were crammed into one humongous building. That meant students had to run in order to reach their classes on time. Olivia looked down at her watch and realized that she only had three minutes until she had to be at her art class. She quickened her pace and started casually running down the Hallway of Terror to her science classroom.

"Excuse me, young lady," called a voice behind Olivia.

The high school math teacher, Mrs. Brown, held up her palm like a stop signal. "No running in the halls, please."

"Yes, ma'am," Olivia said, but she thought, *I don't have time for this*. Then she noticed an enigmatic shape behind Mrs. Brown. It was the cloaked figure she had taken a picture of.

"Thank you." Mrs. Brown smiled as she walked away.

Olivia didn't know if she should chase the cloaked figure or get her phone from Ms. B.'s classroom. Olivia knew that she could always get her phone during lunch, so she chose to follow the mysterious shape. She deduced that the shape was most likely a person. However, she couldn't figure out why that person was there, and, most of all, why they were covering themselves. Were they hiding something?

Olivia followed the shape out of the science wing into the English wing. It seemed like the figure was heading to the basement. All of a sudden, the person in the cloak just stopped moving.

Olivia quickly rushed into the nearest classroom to keep from being seen. *She's going to turn around!* Olivia thought. *I have to get out of here right now!*

Suddenly the hooded figure disappeared into thin air.

Where did she go? Olivia wondered.

"Well, well," cackled a voice from behind her. "Who have we here?"

Olivia's heart skipped a beat. *Who* is *this?* she thought, intimidated. The voice sounded just like the person Agatha was talking to in her office. Olivia slowly turned around, hoping she had just imagined the bone-chilling voice. But her hopes were in vain.

A woman a little shorter than Olivia's dad was seated at a student's desk. She was wearing black gloves and a black hooded cloak. When Olivia looked at the person who was staring at her, her heart stopped cold. There was nothing in that woman's eyes, just black space that seemed powerful enough to suck someone inside and trap them forever.

Olivia tried not to look at them, but they captivated her attention, making her concentrate only on them. There seemed to be some sort of familiarity that drew Olivia in. The rest of the woman's face was quite ugly––witch-like. A skinny, pointy nose was in the center of her face. Olivia squinted in disgust at a small wart at the point of the triangular nose. A single hair sprouted from the center of the wart.

Olivia closed her eyes and opened them again, hoping it was just a dream. But the hooded figure still sat in front of her. Olivia recognized the cloak she had been following in the hall. That could only mean one thing. *I really hope I'm wrong,* Olivia thought. *But I'm probably right.* There was no doubt about it; the lady sitting in front of her was a powerful witch, and her name was Agnes Howler.

10

Where were her friends when she needed them? Olivia looked deep into the face, pushing down the fear that was drowning her mind. Should she call her grandpa for help? *Someone help me!* she exclaimed silently. *Please!* Questions were rushing in and out of her mind. Olivia decided that the quickest solution would be to exit the room. She slowly backed away towards the door, her eyes scanning the witch who sat in front of her, making sure she wouldn't try anything to harm Olivia. Olivia knew it would be a mistake to turn her back on Agnes. After all, she was incredibly dangerous. One powerful spell could probably cause Olivia to crumple to the ground, dead. Olivia didn't trust this woman and didn't want to take her eyes off of her for one second. However, when Olivia tried to open the door, she discovered that it was locked. Of course! There was no way that this witch would let her out of this room so easily. But when Olivia looked into that face, she felt heat run through her body, almost like the woman was familiar with her. That soon turned to harsh coldness. Olivia rubbed her hands together and suppressed a shiver.

"Umm, hello?" Olivia asked. *Is this lady going to talk to me at all? Is she going to hurt me?* Many frightened questions rushed into her mind. She longed for the relaxing comfort of her dad's warm arms. She closed her nervous eyes to wish for that. But it didn't come.

"Scared, are you?" Agnes snickered. "Children!"

Olivia instantly hated this woman. *Why is she even in my school?* Olivia thought helplessly. *She shouldn't be here? Who let her in?* Suddenly, Olivia thought. *Of course! Agatha must have let her in! That traitor!*

I must pretend I'm not scared, Olivia thought. *Maybe then she'll leave me alone.* She took a deep breath and summoned up enough courage to confront Agnes. "I'm not scared," Olivia said, as she tried to stand taller. "What are you doing here?"

"None of your business, child," Agnes said.

Her hollow voice made Olivia wonder why Agnes's

voice was so deep. "How did you get in the building?" Olivia asked, determined to get some answers.

"Ah, so you are a curious girl," the witch replied. "Not how I expected you to turn out."

Olivia was confused. "What are you talking about? This is the first time we've ever met! You don't know me!"

"Oh, the things you don't know, little girl," Agnes's dark voice said.

Olivia didn't like the mysterious vibe this lady was giving her. She pushed the door handle again, but had no luck.

"Let me out." Olivia tugged at the door handle, hoping it would work. "Please." She really didn't like to plead, but she didn't know what else to do. Getting to class was the last thing on her mind; the only thing she wanted was to get out of the presence of the great Agnes Howler. *How am I going to get out!* Olivia thought helplessly. *Should I run for it? But the door is locked! And even if there were other ways to exit the classroom, Agnes probably wouldn't let her leave anyway.*

"Children get frightened so easily," Agnes said coldly. "But don't worry. I won't harm you. After all, I can't hurt you until I'm done with your father."

Olivia's heart stopped cold. How did this woman know her dad? What was going on? Olivia needed to protect him no matter what. "You won't be doing anything to my dad."

Olivia glared at her. "Nothing at all."

"Foolish child," Agnes laughed.

Olivia felt a chill run through her body at that loud cackle. All of a sudden, a wave of anger rushed to her. Now that Olivia knew that Agnes wouldn't harm her, she could yell at her. "If you're going to talk to me, at least say my name instead of calling me child! And stop talking about my dad! He has nothing to do with this! Let me out now or you will pay the price!"

"I'm not so sure about that," Agnes whispered. "A scrawny child is no match for my power!"

"How dare you call me scrawny!" Olivia yelled. "Let me out right this second!"

Agnes sighed. "If I must," Agnes snickered. "But remember, you have not seen the last of me. I am not done with you. The Mystic Pearl is the key to my power. Do not get in my way. Remember, I can hurt you if I want. I stopped Agatha from killing you, but I didn't have to. If you tell anyone about what you've seen here, you're in serious trouble." She paused and added, with a scorn, "Olivia."

Olivia shuddered and pushed down on the handle. The door opened. As she ran out, trying not to think about what was behind her, she heard Agnes's last words.

"I am not done with you yet!"

11

"Are you serious?" Vivian said, after Olivia told her friends what had happened at school. Olivia, Vivian, Dash, and Charles were sitting in Olivia's room.

Olivia leaned back in her chair and sighed. "Yeah, I'm serious," Olivia said, shivering at the thought of the incredibly scary experience. "What do you think my grandpa would say?"

"I'm not really sure," Charles said. "Maybe he'll come and visit you again soon."

"I hope so," Olivia said. Maybe her grandpa could give her more advice. "And…I have something else to tell you guys." Olivia really wanted to tell her friends about her lost brother.

"What?" Vivian said. She and Charles exchanged confused glances. "Is there something wrong?"

I wonder how they're going to react, Olivia thought. "No…just." She took a deep breath. "The Black Death kidnapped Max. That's where he's been for the last two years."

Vivian gasped. "You mean Max, like my brother Max? He's alive?" Her face looked elated.

"Yes, he is," Olivia said. "And I have a brother too. The Black Death kidnapped him when he was just two years old."

Dash looked like he was about to faint. "Surely not? You're not kidding, right?" Dash asked, pulling a hand through his messy hair.

"Of course not!" Olivia exclaimed. "I'd never joke about something like this! The Black Death captured him. That's why he disappeared."

Charles took his glasses off and wiped their lenses with his shirt. "Wow." He smiled as he put his glasses back on. "That's awesomely terrible."

Olivia was really happy that she could share this joy with her friends. "I wonder how Agnes knew all about my dad," Olivia said. "That just doesn't add up to me."

"We need to be really, really careful now," Dash warned. "We know so much. That puts us in great danger!"

Olivia noticed that Vivian was looking a little bit scared. "What's the matter, Vivian?" she asked.

Vivian looked up with worry in her dark brown eyes. "If our brothers have been held captive this whole time, then how could they possibly still be alive? And where have they been?"

Olivia didn't know how to answer Vivian. Then she remembered something else Agnes had mentioned when their paths crossed that morning. "But she won't harm any of us," Olivia assured Vivian.

Charles mouthed something like 'there is no way that can be true.'

"She won't harm us because there is something she wants from my dad," Olivia said.

"How is that even possible?" Vivian sniffled. "She wants us dead."

"Not anymore. I mean, not yet. My dad has something called the Mystic Pearl and Agnes wants it for some reason. She kidnapped our brothers to make my dad give the pearl to her," Olivia said.

"How does the pearl even work?" Vivian asked, looking up with her hand supporting her chin. "What does it do?"

"I have no clue," Olivia said grimly. "But I know it's really important. It is the key to our success, but also the key to our failure."

"That woman is so greedy," Dash said as he shook his head. "She only cares about herself."

"That's for sure," Vivian said. "Can we get a snack?"

Olivia nodded. She and her friends went to the kitchen. There they drank milk and munched on some cookies that Olivia had found in one of the cabinets.

"There's something I don't get," Charles said. "Why hasn't Olivia's dad handed over the pearl for his son?"

That's a good question, Olivia thought. *I wonder why.*

"Agnes might've prevented him," Dash said. "Wait no, trash that, she wants the Mystic Pearl."

"Maybe he's about to? He might have thought we could defeat the Black Death," Vivian said. "But we haven't yet."

"I hope my dad knows us better than that," Olivia said. "He should know that we can get out of a situation like that. But the problem is, Agnes knows powerful magic."

"That makes it a lot harder for us," Dash agreed. "If they were just humans, it would make everything a lot simpler."

"You know, this kinda reminds me of an African folk tale my grandma used to tell me," Charles said.

"What happens?" Olivia asked.

"Well, there are four kids who are faced against an evil queen because they have to rescue their brother to save their world forever," Charles began. "But their brother is the one who has the key to kill the queen. They attempt to save him and. . . ." His voice trailed off.

"Then what happens?" Olivia said.

Charles shook his head. "They fail. The evil queen defeats them."

Olivia raised her eyebrows. *Well, that's dark,* she thought.

"Anyway." Vivian seemed a lot more relaxed now than when she first heard about Olivia's encounter with Agnes. "Are we going to jump in the lake tonight?"

Olivia had completely forgotten about that. Vivian seemed a lot more determined to defeat the Black Death now that she knew her brother would return if they succeeded. "We have to try," Olivia said. "I wonder where it will take us."

PowerSurge finished their snack and started on some homework. Halfway through, Olivia's dad returned home. Last time, he had come back with leaves, dirt, and twigs stuck to his body, and fresh scratches all over him. This time it was worse. He was clutching his ankle, his eyes squinted in pain. His usual beautiful hairstyle was a disaster, all tangled and sprawled haphazardly around his head.

"Dad, what happened? What's been going on? What happened to your ankle? Do you need a bandage?" Olivia worriedly rushed over to him.

"I'll be okay," Olivia's dad yawned. "Now, if you'll excuse me, I just need to take a nap."

"Sure, Dad," Olivia said. She was puzzled as she watched him walk towards his room. She walked back to her friends and sat down.

"What was that about?" asked Dash.

"I have no clue," said Olivia. "But I know he's going crazy."

Suddenly, Vivian screamed louder than Olivia had ever heard her before. She grabbed her backpack and hid her face.

"What?" Charles asked. He looked at the front door and gasped. He too hid his face with his backpack. His pencil case and a few binders fell out of his bag with a loud noise.

"Is that…*Agnes*?" Vivian pointed at the front door that Olivia's dad had left open.

Olivia turned around. She was so shocked to see who was there, she thought her eyes were playing a trick on her.

Agnes stood in the doorway.

"Hello, children," she cackled.

12

Olivia stood up and automatically put out her arms, shielding her friends from the menacing gaze of Agnes Howler.

"How did you find us?" Olivia asked, trying to sound as brave as she could. Part of her was amazed at how powerful Agnes's magic was. "W-w-what are you doing in my house?"

"There are a lot of things about me that would surprise you, child," Agnes said. She raised her foot to step inside the house, but Olivia walked forward.

"Olivia, no," Dash exclaimed. "She's going to hurt you!"

Olivia glanced back at her friends. "She can't, or her

stupid Mystic Pearl will never be in her hands." Olivia's voice sounded a lot more confident than she felt.

"Don't be too sure, Olivia," Agnes snickered.

Olivia felt a shiver pass through her body when Agnes used her real name.

"I can kill you right now if I wanted to!" Agnes said.

"Then do it." Olivia glared at her. She was now only about five feet away from Agnes. Any magic she performed would surely harm Olivia.

"Gladly." Agnes smiled as she raised her cane to strike Olivia with a harmful curse.

Olivia's blood froze. Was she actually going to die now? After everything she had done to keep her promise with her grandpa?

All of a sudden, Agnes's deep eyes turned ice cold. She stared at something behind Olivia. "Miguel," she growled as she slowly lowered her cane.

Olivia sighed in relief. But then she thought, *Why did Agnes stop threatening me when my dad appeared? And how does she know who he is? How does she know his name? In fact, how does she know* my *name? Is there a connection between Agnes and my dad?*

"Agnes," Olivia's dad said. He stood calmly, leaning against the doorway to his bedroom, with his hands in his pockets.

"Yes, it's me." Agnes laughed nervously.

Olivia gasped with surprise. *Was Agnes afraid of her dad? And why was she acting like she knew him?* Olivia wondered if her dad had a secret that involved Agnes. *But what could it be?*

"I still have enough sense to know what you're trying to do." Olivia's dad kept his eyes on Agnes.

Agnes seemed even more scared and surprised. "Always strong, weren't you," she snickered, obviously trying to hide her emotions.

"Get out of my house, now! Leave my daughter alone!" Olivia's dad ordered sternly.

Agnes slowly backed out of the house and pulled her cloak over her head that was filled with evil thoughts. As soon as her face was covered, she just disappeared from view. But before she vanished into the night, her dark, bottomless eyes stared at Olivia as if to say, "I'll be back!"

13

As soon as Agnes was gone, Olivia immediately turned to her dad for an explanation. To her surprise, he wasn't standing in the bedroom doorway anymore. He was already in his bed. *How could he act like everything was normal so quickly? Especially after seeing Agnes,* Olivia thought. *I'm probably going to have nightmares because of the Black Death.* But her dad was sound asleep as if nothing had happened. He definitely wasn't afraid of Agnes, and if he was, he certainly wasn't showing it.

Olivia returned to her friends and sat down beside them.

Vivian opened her mouth to speak, then closed it as

if she didn't know what to say.

"Whoa," Charles whistled. "Definitely a connection there."

Olivia nodded.

"It was like she knew your dad *and* you," Vivian said.

Olivia nodded again. Her friends were right, but she wasn't really listening to them. Anger, determination, confusion, sadness, and fright bubbled inside her. They formed an emotion that was stronger than Olivia had ever felt before. She knew that she, her friends, and her family were in grave danger. She would have to defeat the witches once and for all.

"We have to!" Olivia burst out.

Her friends looked at her with confused expressions.

"I mean, we have to jump into the lake tonight!" Olivia said.

They all nodded.

Suddenly, Dash had an important thought. "Does your dad even know you have a brother?" he asked.

"Probably," Olivia said. "I mean, my brother is his son for heaven's sake. He has to know." She wondered about her brother. She wanted to meet him. She had always envied the relationships Vivian and Dash shared with their brothers.

"I wonder why the Black Death would take Max if

they wanted something from Olivia's dad," Charles said. "Wouldn't it make more sense to take something else from Olivia's dad instead of Max?"

"That's true. But maybe it involved my parents too. And yours," Vivian said, looking at Dash and Charles.

"It's all really complicated," Dash said. "We should probably call our parents to tell them that we won't be home tonight."

"There's no way my mom's going to let me off the hook like that," Vivian said, smiling. "I'll have to sneak out again."

"Dash is right," Charles said. "We have to tell them that we're having dinner somewhere else."

Olivia looked at Charles. "I know it's not polite to self-invite," she said. "But can I come over for dinner?"

Charles laughed at this. "Why are you trying to be polite with your best friends?" he said. "Of course you can come."

"Thanks!" Olivia hugged him. She always loved going to Charles's house for dinner because she loved the meals his mother made. Then she looked at her watch. "We should probably eat now so we can be back in time to jump in the lake."

"And as for homework," Vivian said. "I doubt we'll even be going to school tomorrow."

"Ha! Stupid Agatha Black!" Dash exclaimed. "But

we'll probably be seeing her tonight anyway." His head drooped in disappointment.

"Don't get too excited, Dash," Charles said. "We don't want you to do your full-out victory routine."

Olivia and Vivian laughed. At first, Dash looked a little offended, but in a few seconds, he was laughing along with them.

Olivia wished it could be like this forever. She and her friends were so happy. But they purposely weren't talking about their shared worry. Olivia knew they couldn't avoid it for long before it came to them.

14

It was eleven o'clock and Olivia was lying in her bed. She had about 30 minutes until her friends would get to her house. Had they successfully snuck out? Olivia hoped so. She knew Drake would cover up for Dash if he was the one who caught him, but Deanne definitely wouldn't. Vivian thought she was an only child since Max wasn't considered to be alive, but Olivia's grandpa's recent visit proved otherwise. Charles was an only child and had nobody to cover up for him or catch him, other than his mom. PowerSurge had no clue what to expect, so they planned on bringing the same items they brought into Oak Transport. Olivia tossed over and hugged her stuffed dog, Walter. She didn't know how her friends were going to sneak out of their houses with Agnes on the loose, but she prayed for them to arrive safely. She decided to take a short nap to be refreshed when her friends arrived. She set an alarm for 11:30 and closed her eyes. In a few moments, she opened them again and saw a familiar face.

"Grandpa!" she exclaimed, giving him a hug. He smiled that unmistakable grin with his perfect teeth sparkling like sunlight glazing the snow. *I've missed him so much,* Olivia thought. *I wish he was here all the time!*

"Olivia, you have no idea how proud of you I am right now," he said. "Standing up to Agnes like that, not even flinching when she raised her hand at you. That took sheer courage." He looked like he was about to burst with pride.

Olivia felt elated by the fact that her grandpa was proud of her. That was all she ever strived to do.

"Thanks, Grandpa," she said. "But I need your help." She wanted to ask her grandpa about what she and her friends would find when they jumped in the lake.

Before she could say a word, he raised his hand to stop her. "If you're going to ask me what will happen when you jump in the lake, don't waste your words on that," he said. "I know you can defeat the Black Death. But I can't control what you do or what you will encounter along the way."

Olivia didn't know what to say to that. So she asked another question. "Does this count as your visit to me?" She hoped it wasn't, but judging by the expression on her grandpa's face, she feared it was.

"No, because you didn't call me," he said.

Olivia sighed in relief.

"But remember, when you do call me, I won't be able to answer most of your questions. It's up to you."

"But…but," she said. "Then what's the point?"

Her grandpa stared at her blankly.

"Grandpa, I have a question," Olivia said. "If the witches are capable of such strong magic, can't they just summon us in our sleep and kill us then? They only need *me* to be alive in order to get the pearl, right?

"You might not realize this, Olivia, but you have a stronger connection to magic than you think. That's what has kept you, your friends, and your father alive all this time."

Olivia shook her head. "But how?" she asked.

Her grandpa just smiled his beautiful smile and reached out with his arm. He ruffled Olivia's hair and gave her one last piece of advice that she would need to remember to succeed in this mission. "Just look for the sign in the smoke and you will always find a way."

What does that mean? Olivia thought. *Smoke, a sign?*

Aargh! Why so many mystical terms that don't even make sense?

With that, Olivia's grandpa disappeared.

It was about 11:30 when Olivia's friends showed up. They wore jackets over sweatshirts and many other layers of clothing in order to stay warm.

"My grandpa visited me again," Olivia whispered, as she let them in the house. She told them everything that had happened that night and what she thought her grandpa's advice meant.

"I think it means that we have to do whatever we think is right, no matter what other people say," Vivian said.

"That would make sense," Dash said. "But how is that going to help us?"

There was a moment of silence. Then Charles looked at his watch. "Guys, do we have to leave EXACTLY five minutes before midnight? Because which watch do we look at?"

Olivia remembered what her grandpa told her the first time he visited her.

"We have to look at the watch your dad gave you," she told Charles. "Did you bring it with you?"

Charles smiled.

"We all brought the items we were given," Dash said. "We thought we might need them."

Olivia sighed in relief. She could always count on her friends. "Great thinking, guys," she said. "Why else would they be given to us if we wouldn't need them?"

All of a sudden, a sound came from behind her. "Vivian, pass the flashlight," she said.

Vivian rummaged around in her backpack until she found the flashlight. She handed it to Olivia.

Olivia flicked it on. A black cat was moving around in her own living room. "Guys, look at that!" Olivia exclaimed, pointing at the cat.

Charles frowned. "I don't see anything."

Olivia thought he was crazy until she realized that they probably couldn't see the cat because they weren't in contact with her or the flashlight. "Try touching me," she said.

Her friends put their hands on her shoulders.

Vivian gasped. "Is that cat a shape-shifting witch?" she whispered.

Olivia had never thought that the witches could shape-shift. *Is it a member of the Black Death? Maybe Agnes or Agatha? If so, can they turn into one of my friends or my dad?* Olivia shuddered at the thought of Agnes or Agatha being her dad.

Vivian slowly approached the cat and was about to look into its green eyes.

"Stop!" Dash exclaimed. "Don't look into the eyes.

It might be able to hypnotize you!"

Vivian immediately looked away.

That was a good save by Dash, Olivia thought. *The last thing we need is for one of us to be hypnotized!*

"I can't even see it," Vivian said. "I'm not touching the flashlight anymore."

"Do you think the cat can hypnotize people who can't even see it?" Olivia asked.

Vivian shivered.

"Maybe," Charles said, as he slowly guided Vivian back to her friends. "But better safe than sorry."

Olivia agreed. A scarcely believable thought suddenly came to her. "What if Agnes has hypnotized my dad?" she asked, hoping it wasn't true. *I know it makes sense! But that would mean my dad has seen her before today!* "That would explain why he's acting so strange and secretive!"

Vivian sank down into the black leather of one of Olivia's couches and leaned back into the matching pillows, adjusting her grip on the flashlight. "I really hope not. Do you think he's hiding something?"

Olivia didn't want to answer Vivian's question. She couldn't imagine her dad hiding something from her, and she definitely didn't want to.

"What are we going to do about the cat?" Olivia said to change the subject.

Dash walked to a small closet attached to Olivia's living room. "We need to leave really soon," he said. "For now, this broom will have to do." He picked up a bright red broom. Its bright, white, straw bristles stuck out like a sore thumb.

"Go to the right," Olivia directed him.

Dash slowly moved to his right, holding the broom like a gun that was ready to be fired.

"A little more," Charles told him. "Stop! It's right in front of you."

What surprised Olivia was that the cat seemed so calm as if nothing was happening. It was almost as if it wasn't aware of its surroundings. The cat was just glancing around with its blazing and sparkling green eyes.

Charles opened the front door.

Dash lifted the broom, threatening the cat. The cat merely stood up and casually walked out the door with its tail held high as it disappeared into the darkness of the night.

15

Olivia glanced around nervously at the grim, enormous trees that towered over her head. They were coniferous trees, with many pinecones, creating humongous shadows that kept the forest enveloped in darkness. Sounds were entering Olivia's ears from all directions. Birds were chirping, late at night, preparing to roost, and coyotes were howling, creating vibrations that echoed across the whole forest. But one sound stuck out from the rest. It was a soft and gentle rippling, like the crisp sound of water dripping on a lake. It was relaxing and evened out the rest of the harsh sounds of the mysterious forest. The damp wood chips caused the children's feet to sink into the ground.

Olivia sniffed the humid air around her. The wet scent of pine needles lingered in her nose, causing her to sneeze and break the silence.

"Olivia, Olivia, Olivia." She heard a voice whisper from the darkness.

Olivia looked around. Seeing nothing, she chose to follow the sound of the voice. *Where is that sound coming from?* she wondered. *How does it know my name?*

"This way!" Olivia whispered. She had no reason to, as nobody seemed to be around except her and her friends, but it felt right to whisper. She was following her grandpa's advice and listening to her instinct which was pulling her in one direction.

"Olivia, Olivia, Olivia." She heard the voice whisper again. *I don't like this,* she thought. *It seems a little too...magical.* She motioned for her friends to follow her. A beautiful spectacle surprisingly unfolded before her eyes.

"I see something!" Vivian gasped.

After a few minutes, PowerSurge reached the bank of something unlike anything Olivia had ever seen before. In front of her was a beautiful, starlit lake. It was reflecting the moonlight off of its perfect surface. Its silver water was rippling gently. Olivia's jaw dropped open as she viewed the amazing sight right before her. Her friends stopped beside her as they watched the beautiful lake twinkle in the moonlight. *This is more amazing than anything I've ever seen,* Olivia thought.

"Wow!" Olivia breathed, as she noticed the moon seemed to reflect brighter on the water when she looked at the lake. She wished her dad were there to see the amazing scenery.

All of a sudden, Charles threw his hands up in the air. His sudden movement returned Olivia's mind to the present. She quickly remembered what she needed to do. She turned to ask Charles what time was on his watch, but she was surprised by what she saw. More like, what she *didn't* see.

"Where's Charles?" she asked nervously.

They quickly escaped from the trance of the lake and scanned the dark grounds surrounding them, hoping to catch a glimpse of Charles.

"Charles!" Vivian called. "Where are you?" After no response, Vivian exchanged a worried glance with Olivia.

Where is he? Olivia thought. *I literally just saw him!*

"Maybe he jumped in," Dash said.

Olivia shook her head. "We would have seen him," she said. "There's only one possible explanation. Has Charles been kidnapped just like Max and my brother?"

"Let's not jump to conclusions," Vivian said, shuddering in the cold. "Maybe he just…I'm blanking here. You're probably right, Olivia."

"Do you think this means the Black Death is close by and watching us?" Dash said, crossing his arms.

"It's possible," Olivia said. "It makes sense that if we have to defeat them when we jump in the lake, they're probably going to be here."

"If we jump in, our backpacks will get wet," Dash said. "And our clothes."

You're kidding, right? Olivia thought. *Dash couldn't be thinking about getting wet now! They had more important things to worry about.*

"We have to go on," Vivian said. "That's our only hope of finding Charles. And Max."

Olivia nodded. She was surprised that such brave words came from Vivian. Then Olivia realized that Vivian's brother *and* cousin had been kidnapped. She must be feeling terrible.

"When are we supposed to jump in the lake?" Dash said. "Charles is gone, and that means the watch is too."

Somehow, Olivia thought Charles was smart enough to leave some sort of clue to where he was. She sat down on a tree stump and put her head in her hands to think.

All of a sudden, a flash of light appeared beside the lake. Olivia frowned and stood up. "What's that?" she asked as she cautiously approached the place she saw the light flicker. She crouched down and was surprised to see the watch.

"Is that the watch?" Vivian asked.

Olivia, who was buried deep in her thoughts, was surprised to feel Vivian's warm breath on her ear.

Dash ran towards Olivia and Vivian. "No way!" he exclaimed. "I knew Charles would leave us a clue!"

Olivia couldn't believe their luck. Charles must have secretly taken it off so his friends could jump in the lake at the right time. Olivia was glad that Charles was so smart. But when she looked at the hands on the watch, her heart skipped a beat.

"We're late!" she whispered. "No!"

The clock had just ticked past midnight. Her friends were silent.

We haven't even really started our mission! Olivia thought helplessly.

"After all this!" Dash sighed.

Vivian took a deep breath. "We can't be," she said. "We have to try." Turning to Olivia, she added, "Your grandfather would want us to."

Olivia nodded. A thought rushed into her head. "What if we rewind the clock?" she said. "Do you think that would work?"

"It's worth a try," Dash said.

Olivia placed her trembling fingers on the knob of

the watch. She slowly turned it backward and set the watch to one minute before midnight. *What will happen if we jump in at the wrong time?* She decided it was best to not speak her thoughts.

Olivia's friends followed her to the rim of the sparkling lake.

Dash held the watch. His blue eyes carefully followed each movement of the ticking hand.

Olivia shivered and hugged her arms. The lake looked like it could easily give her frostbite if she dipped in one finger.

"Ten seconds," he warned Olivia and Vivian.

I'm so nervous! Olivia thought. *What if it doesn't work?* She took a deep breath. "Five." She tightened her backpack straps around her shoulders and clenched her fists.

"Four," Vivian said.

Olivia slowly blinked.

"Three," Dash said.

Olivia dragged her foot across the dirt ground. "Two," Olivia said, taking a deep breath.

"One." Olivia had no time to think before she heard the next word.

"JUMP!" Dash shouted.

Olivia took a huge gulp of air and sank into the lake. The freezing-cold water wrapped around her threateningly. She and her friends had jumped into the lake. It would lead them to the answers to all of their questions, but if they weren't careful, they would never come back.

16

Olivia tightly shut her eyes as she felt a strange sensation spread through her body. *I feel so calm,* she thought. *Almost as if I'm the only person in the world.* But suddenly, she felt the cold water floating around her body. *This water is so cold!* she thought. She was slowly drifting down into the magical lake, holding onto every bit of air as if it was her last lifeline. Was something supposed to be happening? It just seemed like jumping into an ordinary lake. She slowly opened her eyes. To her surprise, although she and her friends were still in the water, they could open their eyes to see as easily as if they were on land. Bubbles were forming all around her in the dark, midnight blue water. She grasped her heaving chest in agony. In seconds, she would run out of air and suffocate under the water. After holding her breath longer than she had ever attempted, she fell unconscious.

Olivia felt burning pain pierce her body as she woke up on sharp, rocky ground. She slowly opened her eyes and was surprised to see many cuts across her arms and legs. The rocks were sharp enough to inflict wounds. There was fresh blood welling up around the cuts. When she turned over, she felt a sharp pain. A long, thin cut ran from her elbow to her hand. Fresh blood was staining her arm a deep red.

"Oww!" she cried. Two eyes connected with hers, and she saw the comforting shape of her grandpa. *Grandpa?* she wondered. *Again?*

"It's okay," he said gently as he calmed her down.

He sounded so young, as if he had returned to her age again. Olivia blinked. It wasn't her grandpa in front of her; it was Dash.

He motioned to Vivian to come forward.

Vivian had cut a piece of her own pants, and wrapped it around Olivia's arm.

Olivia winced. "It hurts," she said. She slowly sat up. Her tense body immediately relaxed as she met Vivian's soft gaze.

"You'll be okay," Vivian said. She slowly helped

Olivia up to her shaking feet.

Olivia eagerly looked around at her surroundings. Just a few feet in front of her was a river. However, this definitely wasn't a normal river. Burning hot lava was flowing in it. Looking at the bright-orange substance made Olivia instantly feel hot. She immediately removed her jacket. When she looked up to see the source of the lava, she was astonished to see a volcano towering far over her head. It was a dirty brown color. A stream of lava flowed down the steep side and formed the lava river. She read the words that had been raggedly carved into the ground. '*Here lies River Magmus.*' Looking around, she noticed that the world was bare of plants. Almost everything was black and brown, except for the flaming-hot, red-and-orange lava. Cave-like buildings were spread along the lava river. Holes had been cut into the tops of the structures and filled with glass windows. *What* is *this place?* Olivia thought, alarmed.

"Where are we?" she asked. Looking at her friends, she knew she wouldn't get much of an answer—they looked just as surprised as she was.

"I dunno," Dash said. "Somewhere weird for sure."

Olivia and Vivian nodded in agreement. Scanning her eyes over the caves, Olivia couldn't help but think that this place was connected to the Black Death.

"How did we get here from the lake?" Vivian asked. "And why aren't we underwater anymore?"

That's a good question, Olivia thought. *How?*

"I don't know," Dash said. "Magic, I guess."

That made sense. After all, they *were* dealing with witches.

"Let's explore!" Olivia exclaimed. She eagerly led her friends into the unknown world in front of them.

Walking right beside the caves gave Olivia chills, so she led her friends away from them.

After a few minutes of looking around, Dash's excitement bubbled up to where he couldn't hold it in anymore. "Let's go in one!" he burst out.

Olivia and Vivian looked at him curiously.

"One of the cave things," he explained.

Olivia shared a nervous look with Vivian. They had only been in this weird place for a few minutes, and Dash was already willing to take risks.

"I don't know," Vivian said. "We don't know anyone here, and it might not be safe. Actually, scratch that. It *definitely* won't be safe."

Olivia agreed with her. However, her heart skipped a beat when Dash said, "Maybe Charles is in one of them."

Vivian inhaled deeply. She was obviously scared for her cousin's safety.

"It's possible," Olivia said. "But how are we going to get him out if it is the Black Death who kidnapped him? Plus, we'd have to search every single cave. There are so many of them!"

Dash's eyes grew wider. He obviously hadn't thought about that factor.

"We should try," Vivian said. "For Charles's sake."

Olivia nodded. Even though it was dangerous, she knew Vivian was right.

"How are we going to get in?" Dash asked. "There are no doors to enter the caves." He had a point. There was no way to enter the structures that Olivia could see.

"There has to be some way to get in," Olivia said. "If not, how would the witches enter the caves themselves?" Suddenly, she recalled what had happened during her first encounter with Agnes Howler. She had teleported herself through the classroom walls.

"They're witches," Vivian said. "They're bound to use some sort of magic to get in."

Olivia's inquisitive eyes scanned the dark caves. "Maybe there is some type of underground tunnel that will get us to the caves!" she said.

Dash nodded his approval. "That would make sense," he said. "In case the witches have a visitor who doesn't know magic."

Vivian looked like she agreed. "Let's try it," she said.

With that, the three friends set out on a dangerous mission, either to emerge victorious or never to return home again.

17

"Let's head towards the volcano," Olivia said. After speaking, she instantly regretted it. Looking up at the enormous volcano, she felt goosebumps run down her spine. *How could something this big be created? Is science different in this world?* she wondered. Thinking back to a science unit about volcanoes, another question entered her mind. *Are there any tectonic plates here? But as far as we know, we're not even on earth. And all the volcanoes on earth are much smaller than this one!* She couldn't even see the top of the volcano, or even halfway up.

Vivian shuddered at the sight.

Dash looked down nervously. "Maybe there's

another way to get in the tunnel, assuming there is one?" he said.

Olivia immediately looked around. Spotting a large plant sticking out in plain sight, Olivia smiled.

"These witches may be powerful," she said. "But they sure aren't very smart." Rushing towards the plant, she turned to her friends. "Remember what we found last time we saw a plant?"

Dash and Vivian laughed. They took their places beside the plant to help Olivia move it.

"Three…two…one…. Push!" Vivian said.

Olivia, Dash, and Vivian pushed with all their might, revealing a black trapdoor.

Olivia brushed some dirt off of the square and grabbed its handle. *Is this the tunnel?*

"You can do the honors," Olivia stepped back to let Dash open the door.

Dash smiled at her and came forward. He opened the trapdoor with a loud creak.

Olivia cringed at the sound. Looking into the space the trapdoor had protected, Olivia shrieked. She couldn't see anything. The space was in complete darkness. Even with the blazingly bright volcano and lava river by it, there was still no light reflected inside.

"Whoa," Vivian gasped. "Who's going in first?" She and Olivia both looked at Dash.

"Hey, why are you looking at me?" Dash asked. "Ladies first!"

Olivia shook her head and smiled. *Not in this case, scaredy-cat!* she thought.

"Okay, fine, I'll go first," Dash sighed.

"We don't know how deep it will be, so be careful," Olivia warned him.

Dash nodded and sat down on the edge of the opening. "Wait, there's a ladder!" he said. Putting his feet on the first rung, he slowly climbed down. There was a thud when his feet touched the ground.

Olivia knew the tunnel must be pretty far down, as Dash's voice was very faint.

"It's good! Not too deep actually." Dash called from below. "The tunnel roof is about a foot taller than me!"

"I'll go next," Olivia said. She poised herself to jump in. She slid her legs down through the opening and felt them hit the first rung of the ladder.

"You're good!" Dash called.

Olivia climbed down the ladder and touched down on the ground. She was standing on a soft, mushy substance that felt wet, like dirt. She couldn't see what was ahead of her. The only light was a very dim glow from the open trapdoor. She took her backpack off her shoulders and felt around for the zipper. She opened the backpack and took out her regular flashlight. It didn't have any powers; it just made light. As soon as she illuminated it, Dash shielded his eyes from the sudden light.

"Olivia, turn that off!" he exclaimed, covering his squinted eyes with his hands. "The light is so bright!"

Olivia turned the flashlight off and helped Vivian down into the tunnel. Then Olivia shut the trapdoor, and she and her friends were left in complete darkness.

18

Olivia couldn't see ten inches in front of her. Although she knew it would bother Dash, she turned her flashlight back on. *Okay, we're not going to get anywhere without the light,* she thought. *He knows we need it.* This time, Dash didn't object, but merely looked away.

"Which way do we go?" Vivian asked.

Looking around, Olivia realized that they were standing in the middle of an intersection. There were three possible ways they could go. "There has to be a clue!" Olivia exclaimed. "Or else the witches might not get past here themselves." She looked both ways to see if there was a clue somewhere.

"I think we just have to choose one," Dash said. "It's like guess and check."

Yeah, but not a math problem, Olivia thought. *This time, we're the ones in the math problem. It's like life or death!*

He walked in one direction, but then returned to his friends. "What happens if we go the wrong way?"

"I'm thinking that this is some sort of underground maze, so that intruders can't get to the caves so easily," Olivia said.

"If we hit a dead end, maybe there will be a key or some sort of riddle or question we have to answer," Vivian said.

"That's true," Dash said. Suddenly, his face lit up. "We should leave a trail so that if we hit a dead end, we can find a way back! Like Theseus did with the ball of string in the Greek tale about Daedelus's Labyrinth! And Hansel and Gretel!"

"That's a great idea!" Olivia exclaimed. "But what can we use?"

Vivian opened her backpack. "I brought some White Rabbit Candy," she said as she pulled out a huge plastic bag full of them. "My mom brought boxes full when she came back from China last month. We could use them."

Dash nodded and took the bag from Vivian. He slid

the zipper open and placed his hand inside. Instead of marking their starting point, he popped one in his mouth.

Dash! Olivia thought. *Not the time!*

"Mmm," he sighed as he munched noisily on the candy. "These are really, really good. Where did your mom buy them?"

Olivia and Vivian both glared at him.

"Okay, okay, I'll stop!" Dash closed the bag.

Olivia put her hand out. "Hand them over," she told Dash. "We can't trust you with food resources."

"Okay fine," Dash grumbled as he placed the bag in Olivia's hand. "But I was hungry."

Vivian sighed. "We can eat later," she told him. "Let's just get into the caves now." Vivian took the bag of White Rabbit Candy, opened it, and dropped one candy where they were standing. Turning to her friends, she said, "Which way?"

Olivia pointed to their left. They started walking in that direction. Olivia was in front holding the flashlight, while Vivian was behind her, dropping candy along the way. Dash was at the back, just trying to steal the candies from Vivian's bag. Olivia could hear his stomach grumbling quietly as they walked. After a few minutes of walking, they hit another intersection.

"Now which way?" Vivian asked.

Dash pointed to the right.

They went right. When they crossed another intersection, this time, they walked straight ahead. However, they soon hit a dead end.

"Oh no!" Olivia exclaimed. "It's fine, we'll just turn around." But surprisingly, when she tried to go back, she found a huge gate. *How had that gate appeared in such a short time?* Olivia hadn't even heard anything. Her heart skipped a beat when she heard a voice behind her.

"You have reached a dead end. Solve the riddle to escape."

Who's there? she thought. Olivia slowly turned around, expecting to see someone. Instead, she found a small piece of paper lying on the dirt floor. She breathed out with relief when she realized the voice was just a recording. The witches seemed to be playing games with them.

"You were right!" Dash said to Vivian. "We do have to solve a riddle to get out!"

Vivian was standing beside the gate, shivering.

Olivia remembered with a start that Vivian was afraid of dark spaces. That was the reason why she had been so apprehensive and reluctant to enter Oak Transport. Olivia walked over to Vivian. "You'll be okay," Olivia put her arm around Vivian to calm her down.

Vivian inhaled deeply. "I know," Vivian told her. "But all of the drama with the witches makes it ten times worse."

Olivia nodded understandingly.

Vivian shook her head. "Anyway, we have to get back to work."

Olivia walked over to the piece of paper and crouched down to pick it up. She read the ragged handwriting scribbled all over it.

"Sarah has four daughters," she read, squinting because the handwriting was so hard to read. "Each of them has a brother. How many children does Sarah have?" Olivia turned to her friends. The first answer that popped up in her head was eight. *That has to be wrong,* Olivia thought. *It's too easy. This has to be a trick question!*

"Isn't it just five?" Dash asked after thinking for a few seconds. "If they're siblings, they share the same brother."

"That sounds right," Olivia said. "But where do we say the answer to get out of here?"

They all looked around for some type of device that would acknowledge their answer and let them go past the gate. Olivia moved her flashlight slowly around the small space.

"Look!" Vivian called. "I found something!"

Olivia and Dash looked at what Vivian had found —a small speaker embedded into the dirt floor.

Dash bent down to say his answer into it. "Five!" he yelled.

The whole ground vibrated as the metal gate loudly creaked open onto a wide space, allowing PowerSurge to exit the cramped area. Olivia led her friends away from where they had been trapped. PowerSurge followed the trail of candy that Vivian had left behind. Vivian picked up each piece and followed Olivia.

"Here's the last intersection we passed," Dash said when they reached an intersection that split into two ways. "We have to go the other way."

Olivia nodded. This time, they went right instead of left. After a few more minutes of walking, they reached another intersection.

Olivia remembered a trick that her dad had taught her a long time ago. "Lick your finger and hold it up," she said. "You can feel which way the wind is blowing on your finger. In this case, it's heat." *There won't be any wind because of the Lava River,* Olivia thought.

"I think it's left," Dash said.

Vivian frowned. "Are you sure?" she asked him. "I feel it's right."

They both turned to ask Olivia which one of them was right.

Olivia held up her finger to test it for herself. "I also think it's right," she said. "But barely."

Vivian nodded and dropped a piece of candy at the intersection and they went right.

"What's that smell?" Vivian asked, fanning her nose. "It's really bad!"

Olivia stopped to smell the air and plugged her nose. "I'm not sure," she said.

Dash pulled his shirt up to cover his nose. "Are we going the right way?" he asked.

Suddenly, Olivia heard a low growl from around the corner. A large shadow appeared on the left wall of the cave. A large monster emerged from the shadow, stopping Olivia in her tracks. Standing in front of her was a large beast, three times the size of Dash, Vivian, and Olivia put together. It had dark, sleek skin, almost blending in completely with the wall. The first thing that Olivia noticed was that the creature had five heads, joined together on one neck, performing every movement as one. Its bloodshot red eyes were shining brightly in the muddy tunnel as Olivia and her friends cringed together in fear. *Who is this creature?* Olivia thought. *Where did he come from?*

"H-h-hello?" Olivia shuddered.

The beast did something that looked like it was trying to smile.

Does it have a voice? Olivia wondered. *Does it understand English, or does it only speak a language that the witches share?*

"Foolish." The beast growled an answer to her question. "My name is Magma, child of the holy River Magnus."

Olivia thought it was weird to call that menacing lava river 'holy.'

"Can we move past you, please?" Vivian asked, trying to be polite to the dangerous creature.

Dash merely nodded.

"Stupid child," Magma laughed.

Olivia's insides burned at the fact that something had called her friend stupid. *He's just like Agnes!* Olivia thought.

She slowly leaned closer to her friends. "Here's the plan," she whispered. "We need to find his weakness. My guess is that he has one weak spot, somewhere on his gigantic body. We need to know where that spot is to beat him."

Vivian nodded.

"Kind of like Achilles's Heel," Dash whispered.

Olivia smiled. "Exactly," she whispered. "Let's do this!"

They picked up some dirt from the bottom of the tunnel and threw it at Magma. The creature laughed.

To their surprise, the dirt seemed to bond with him, just making him bigger. *How is this even happening?* Olivia thought fearfully.

"You think that can harm the mighty Magma!" he cried. "WRONG!"

Olivia looked around, but didn't see anything that might harm Magma. In fact, all she saw was dirt.

Magma started ambling towards them. He crouched down and picked up a handful of dirt. He flung it at Olivia with all his might.

Olivia ducked. The dirt narrowly missed her head. She heard a thud as it collided with the ground behind her. She narrowed her eyes at the demon.

"You're going down!" she yelled. She signaled to her friends to pick up some more dirt to throw it at the same time. She felt the dirt slide off her sweaty fingers as she threw it with all her might.

However, the dirt had no impact on Magma. He stayed where he was—not even flinching.

Olivia wasn't ready to give up yet. She knew that everything had a weakness, whether it was obvious or not. There had to be something that could harm this creature, whether it would kill him or not. She quickly devised a plan. She wasn't sure if it would work, but she knew that she had to try or she would never forgive herself.

Olivia stopped moving completely, pretending that she was frozen.

"Scared, are you?" Magma laughed. "Nobody can defeat me!"

Olivia wished her friends knew what her plan was, but she had no opportunity to tell them. After she stood still for twenty more seconds, they started to catch on. Obviously, they couldn't read minds and didn't know exactly what she was thinking, but they knew to follow her moves. She crept slowly towards Dash, waiting five seconds between every step.

Vivian realized that Olivia might want her to distract the demon, so she did.

"Dash, the eagle cart," Olivia whispered when she finally reached him.

Dash opened his backpack as quietly as he could. "Are you sure you want to use it?" he whispered. "We can only use it once."

"Have any better ideas?" she whispered. *I know we can't kill this beast, but we can still try to escape,* she thought.

Vivian was desperately throwing dirt at Magma's face, trying to divert his attention away from Dash and Olivia.

Dash handed the eagle cart to Olivia.

Olivia felt an awkward sensation flow through her body as the tiny object was placed in her hands. She examined the sled held in the air by two large eagles with blue eyes.

Dash gently took the cart back from her. "My mom told me that I'm the only one who has the power to activate it," he explained.

Olivia nodded.

Dash began the process of enlarging the magic toy. He placed it in his hand and closed his eyes. He seemed to be doing some type of prayer.

Suddenly Olivia noticed the cart was growing. Vivian was still flinging dirt at Magma, but Olivia could see she was getting tired. Olivia rushed over to help Vivian throw more mud at Magma. Olivia knew that the tactic wouldn't work for much longer—it was just making Magma bigger. But they had to buy time. The eagle cart was now only a little too small for the kids to fit inside.

Olivia rushed back over to Dash. "Come on Dash!" she whispered. "You can do it."

Dash barely acknowledged that he heard her and shut his eyes tighter. All of a sudden, he exhaled loudly and opened his eyes.

"It's ready," he whispered. "Jump aboard!"

He did it! Olivia thought. *Now we can get away from*

this beast! Olivia hopped in the eagle cart. Dash got in beside her.

"Vivian!" Olivia yelled. "Over here!"

That shout caught Vivian's attention—as well as Magma's. Vivian put her arm down, exhausted. Magma started moving towards the eagle cart. But Vivian was too quick for him. She sprinted with all of the energy she had left, and reached her friends seconds before Magma.

"Great job, Vivian!" Dash exclaimed. "Fly out of the maze," he ordered the eagle cart.

Only now could Olivia look at the cart and take in its beautiful features. The cart was a bright-red, outlined with silver pearls. The seats were made of plush leather, enlightened with white. There was a trunk, almost big enough for another person. *This sort of reminds me of Santa's sleigh,* Olivia thought, remembering the real world, or at least its tales.

The cart zoomed up into the sky. Olivia could feel the air rushing against her face.

But their proud victory was short-lived. Magma hadn't given up yet. With one step, he reached the eagle cart, raised one of his powerful fists, and struck one of the eagles.

"No!" Vivian yelled as the eagle fell.

The eagle was still attached to the cart, so he hung

there, adding weight for the one remaining eagle.

Olivia knew what she had to do. She reached into her backpack and grabbed the rope she had thought she might need on the trip. She tied one end to her waist and the other to one of the posts on the cart. Jumping with careful aim, Olivia landed right on the injured eagle's back. There was a huge gash on its wing. He was barely able to carry her, so Olivia put most of her weight on the rope that was tied to her waist. Olivia cut the tie between the eagle and the cart, so the other eagle didn't have to carry the injured one as well. Olivia didn't feel stable on the back of the eagle, so she held her arms out to steady them. She could feel the cart quickly descending because there was too much weight for one eagle to carry. Though it would be dangerous, Olivia knew what she had to do.

"Cut the rope!" she yelled to her friends above.

She could just make out Dash's worried reply. "It's too dangerous!" he shouted.

Olivia saw the cart was sinking faster. She tried desperately to persuade Dash. "Please!" she begged. "For me! I'll be fine! I promise!"

Dash took a deep breath and nodded. He untied the rope from the post on the cart.

Olivia felt a rushing wind as she and the eagle plummeted to the ground at deadly speed.

19

Olivia was about to fatally crash into the dirt ground. Then, at the last second, a miracle happened. A strong wind magically swept her away from the ground. It safely carried her out of the maze to where the tunnel ended. Olivia breathed out in relief and took a few minutes to recover from the experience she just had.

"Olivia, are you good?" Dash's voice came from behind her.

She jerked back to the present. When she looked up, she realized that she was sitting on a bumpy dirt path that led to a cliff.

Olivia stood up and cautiously walked towards the edge of the cliff. She stared down at a view that she had never expected to find. She was looking over a large underground city, full of many flat-topped, circular homes. The caves had balconies and they were stacked on top of each other in a precarious way. They were a darkish brown color, made of dirty-looking rock. The stacks of caves were separated with narrow alleyways lit by free-standing lanterns. It was nighttime, and it felt odd to look up into the sky and see no moon there. Instead, the city was bright due to the luminous glow of the lava river. Olivia felt her body warm at the sight of the heat. Olivia immediately knew that this city was the home of the Black Death, the deadly witch gang that she and her friends had to defeat. She also had a feeling that Charles was imprisoned in one of the caves, being held captive for the Mystic Pearl. *This place may be full of evil, but it sure is beautiful in its own unique way,* she thought.

"Whoa!" she breathed out. "This is amazing!"

Dash and Vivian nodded their agreement.

"Definitely," Vivian said. "But incredibly dangerous at the same time. Don't forget the witches want us dead and will do anything to make that come true. We have to be on the watch at all times and avoid any living creature."

Looking below at the gloomy but lit city, Olivia wondered. *Did any other animals live in the Witches'*

World besides the witches themselves?

"I wonder which one Charles is in?" Dash said. The eagle cart was once again miniature. He put it in his backpack and slung it over his shoulder.

"The eagle!" Olivia gasped. She couldn't believe she had been so selfish and not even thought about the hurt eagle.

Dash smiled. "Classic Olivia," he sighed. "Don't worry. He's safe. My mom's spirit came and restored his body."

Olivia sighed with relief. *I feel bad for that poor eagle,* she thought. *He was only trying to help us.*

"Hey, do you think she's the one who powered the magical wind that saved me?" Olivia asked.

"I guess that's possible," Dash said. "After all, it was pretty magical."

"What now?" Vivian asked. "We have no idea which cave Charles is in. Or if he is even here!"

Olivia and Dash looked at each other.

"What do we always do?" Dash asked.

"Explore!" they all chimed together.

Olivia stood proudly on the cliff, feeling powerful as its shadow loomed over the city. Suddenly, her eye noticed something. It was quite far away, but she instantly could tell it was absolutely enormous. It was the only white object in the city that she could see, and the only glimpse of the modern world. *That's so out of place here!* she thought. *It must be vital to the city.*

"What's that?" Olivia asked, pointing at the structure.

Her friends turned to look at it.

Vivian squinted and laid her hand across her forehead to get a better look. "I'm not sure," she said. "But it must be important."

Olivia nodded in agreement.

"Now let's go rescue Charles!" Dash exclaimed, putting his hand out so it was in the middle of all of them.

Vivian placed her hand on top of his. "You in, Olivia?" she asked.

Olivia smiled. "Always," she said, putting her hand on Vivian's. But looking over the dangerous city in which their important mission would take place, she suddenly didn't feel so sure.

20

Olivia was sitting on a sharp, small boulder that jutted out from the rocky surface of the cliff that overlooked the city. She peered down from the tall cliff, shuddering at the thought of her body tumbling down the rough side, losing every single bit of life left inside. She shifted when a piercing pain flashed through her body. The rock she was sitting on had many sharp, pointy edges. Staring over the city reminded Olivia of all the malevolent witches that were out to harm her and her friends.

"Do you think the witches know we're here?" Olivia said.

Vivian looked at her, her eyes dark with shadows. "I

hope not," she said. "Or else."

Olivia nodded in agreement. She didn't really want to hear the end of Vivian's sentence.

"How would they know we were here?" Dash asked. "Oh, wait, they have powers."

To Olivia, it seemed like Dash hadn't thought through the fact that the witches were magical.

"We have to get some sort of disguise," Vivian said. "There are witches flying over the city."

The sky was darkening and River Magmus was adding a luminescent glow to it.

"They'll be sure to recognize us if we don't," Dash said. His head drooped below his sinking shoulders; he was exhausted after the long day.

"But where are we supposed to find something to use?" Olivia asked. Her eyes scanned their surroundings, looking for something they could make into a disguise. "I don't see anything here."

"We might be able to find something in one of the caves," Vivian said. "But we have to be really careful sneaking in."

Olivia nodded and gazed over the sprawling city beneath her. All of a sudden, she felt so powerful, as if she was in control of everything, and that there was no way the witches could defeat her.

"I'm really tired," Dash yawned. He closed his eyes

halfway, hoping to get a chance to sleep.

"We can take turns keeping watch," Vivian said.

Olivia nodded. "I'll take the first shift," Olivia said. She wasn't ready to sleep yet. *I know I'm exhausted, but I probably won't be able to sleep, with so much being on my mind,* she thought. Looking over the lit city made Olivia think of her grandpa. She wondered if he was proud of her. "I love you, Grandpa!" she whispered to the night sky. "I hope you're proud of me!" Though this wasn't her world, Olivia strongly felt as if her precious grandpa was still watching over her.

"Dash," Olivia whispered, shaking his shoulders lightly. "It's time to wake up!"

Dash mumbled and turned over.

Olivia sighed. There was no way she could wake him. Whenever he was asleep, he wouldn't wake up unless he wanted to. She had barely gotten any sleep, but she had felt too guilty to wake Dash after seeing him so tired. Vivian had taken one shift, and Olivia covered for Dash, only fitting in two or three hours of sleep for herself. She yawned, suddenly feeling tired. *Why is it that when I'm supposed to sleep, I can't, but when I'm not supposed to, I feel like sleeping,* Olivia thought, annoyed with herself.

"Leave me alone," Dash grumbled. "I'm sleeping."

Olivia sighed. *That's been pretty obvious to me for a while,* she thought. "It's been eight hours," she said.

"WHAT!" Dash suddenly jerked up with an extremely surprised look on his face. Then he pointed to the city. "Oh my gosh, the witches are flying down there!"

Olivia laughed. "Well, yeah, that was going on a long time ago, Dash," she said. "Which ones do you think they are?" She couldn't recognize the bony body of Agatha, or the thin but muscular body of Agnes. Olivia glanced over her shoulder at Vivian who sat close to the edge of the cliff, looking out at the city below them. There were three witches flying on canes that Olivia could see, which was surprising. Ever since she saw Agnes disappear on the magical cane, she thought that witches on canes would be invisible. Maybe they weren't because they were in their own world where nobody could see them. At least, that's what they thought.

"How are we going to get down?" Vivian asked.

Olivia's body lurched. She hadn't realized Vivian was beside her.

"Eagle cart?" said Dash.

Olivia shook her head. "Already used it. How about my rope?" she asked. "It sure is coming in handy on this trip. We can use it more than once. It's not magical."

Vivian and Dash looked at each other.

"Sorry," Dash said, glancing at his feet. "It was lost when you came out of the maze. Plus, it wouldn't be very safe at all."

Olivia sighed.

Dash stormed around her and stomped his foot twice in frustration. Suddenly, the ground opened up below him. He quickly fell into a hole and disappeared.

"Dash!" Vivian exclaimed, rushing to the spot where he had been.

Olivia followed close behind.

"What happened?" Vivian asked.

Looking down the chute where Dash had disappeared, Olivia grinned. "I think Dash might've accidentally found the way down," she said.

"You go next," Vivian said.

Olivia nodded and jumped in the chute. She felt all of the air being forced from her lungs as she slid down the dark space. She was going at top speed, with her hands crossed over her chest in the safest position. All of a sudden, she felt her feet touch the ground and she crashed onto the floor in a dizzy mess.

"You made it!" Dash whispered. "I accidentally found the way down!"

Olivia opened her eyes and stumbled onto her feet. A loud thump told her that Vivian had touched down too. After helping Vivian up to her feet, Olivia looked at her surroundings. She was standing in a kitchen. It had to belong to one of the witches, but Olivia expected it would be a little more dark looking. Its gray cabinetry was polished with golden knobs and mounted along the walls in an orderly fashion. A big island was placed in the center of the kitchen, containing an old-fashioned gas stove. It had a black countertop, shining with its bright obsidian surface. There were three chairs tucked under the island, dark black with an outline of silver pearls. A window was letting the natural light flow into the room. Because the ceiling was arched, Olivia assumed that she was in one of the structures she had seen from the cliff earlier.

"Is it just me, or do you guys also feel like something terrible is about to happen?" Olivia asked. "I don't have a good feeling about this place."

Her friends nodded in agreement.

"It's not just you," Dash said. "Any place relating to the witches gives me that feeling." He looked around and shuddered in discomfort.

"Do you guys think this is Agatha's house?" Vivian questioned, taking a seat in one of the chairs.

"I doubt it," Olivia said. "Her house was in Oak Transport, remember?"

"That could have been her workspace, but maybe

her real home is here," Dash said.

"It's possible," Olivia said. "But we'd better find a closet to look for a disguise." *I think we're going to have to dress up as witches,* she thought. *I don't want to be a witch!*

The three friends looked around the kitchen. They hoped to find something that would provide cover for them when they were sneaking through the Witches' World.

Olivia noticed a staircase leading to a locked door. It was probably the door to the home of another of the witches, connected to this one which was stacked below.

"Let's try the bedroom," Dash said. "Maybe we'll find something there."

They headed in the direction in which they expected to find the bedroom. Instead, they found a living room that was filled with dark decor. A large cuckoo clock was sitting on the black mantle which was above the lit fireplace. There were two black-leathered couches resting on either side of the room. In between them was a beautiful circular table made of polished glass. Finally, a brown armchair was placed on the side of the room, lit with a bright grey free-standing lamp. This living room was so different from Olivia's style; she preferred bright colors to bring happiness to the house. She was about to walk past the living room when something caught her eye. She noticed a chest tucked into the corner of the room, as if the owner forgot about it or was hiding it from guests. She strolled over to it, curious to see what it contained.

Olivia motioned for Vivian and Dash to come over to her.

"What's that?" asked Vivian.

"I'm not sure," Oliva said. "It's some sort of chest." *What could be inside here?* she thought. *We're probably not supposed to know if the owner hid it in a chest.*

The reddish-brown chest intrigued them as they examined its bright-golden handle, silver pearls, and soft material. There was something extremely fascinating about it. It just looked out of place—like it shouldn't be there, or it was hiding something.

"Should we open it?" asked Dash.

Vivian looked a little bit nervous. "Should we really be opening someone else's property?" she asked, looking around. "In fact, we shouldn't really be here in the first place."

Deep down, Olivia agreed. But her curious side wanted to explore. "Sorry, Vivian, but I think it's okay," Olivia said. "We won't take anything from inside it. Unless we find something that can help us. Like a disguise."

Dash nodded.

"Okay." Vivian sighed. "But don't blame me if we get in trouble."

Dash quickly placed his hand on the golden handle and opened the chest. A loud squeaking noise came from its three large, brass hinges.

Looking at the contents of the chest, Olivia felt her heart open towards its owner. It was filled with diaries, stories, and pictures of people.

"That's cool," Olivia whispered.

Dash reached in the chest before Olivia could stop him.

Vivian shook him by his shoulders. "Dash!" she exclaimed. "Not ours, remember?"

"What?" he said. "It might help us find Charles."

Olivia nodded.

Dash took out one of the diaries. It was so old that the brown leather cover had ripped in a few places, even though it was highly durable. The pages had yellowed with age, and the whole diary seemed very delicate.

"Read it," Vivian said. She clearly had forgotten about her earlier opinion and now was very curious about the contents.

Dash carefully opened the diary and started reading.

Monday, October 14th, 1991, (Or is it October 15th?)

Hello. I am Raven Shadow. I'm nine years old and I go to Walter Bryce Elementary School. I have a cat. He is the cutest little thing ever! His name is Magma, named after lava because I really like hot things. Also, I have a secret. I can't tell any of my friends because my mom told me not to. Here it is: My whole family are witches! I never grew up around boys so we are all witches. I think my mom is very important in her gang. It is called the Black Death or something like that. She doesn't tell me much because I think she doesn't trust me. Her name is Dolores Dark. She is very pretty. You might think that it's weird that I have a different last name than my mom, but that's just how witches work. Every witch has their own first and last name. It's too bad that I don't know any magic. I wish I could cast a spell to get free candy all the time. But my mom doesn't let me have candy. She doesn't even let me go to my friends' houses or anything! I hate my mother! I wish she would be nicer to me. She just thinks that I'm a silly kid who got in the way of her witchcraft life. But one day, I'll show her who's really boss!

Dash took a deep breath.

"She went to OUR school?" Olivia said. "No way!" She leaned back, completely surprised by what she had just heard.

"Do you think there are more witches who went to our school?" Dash asked.

That makes sense, Olivia thought. *If Raven came to*

Walter Bryce Academy, then maybe other witches did too.

"Keep reading," Vivian urged Dash. "There might be a picture of the witches. Then we would know if some of them teach at our school!"

Dash flipped the page and started reading. "Wait, what?" he said. "This doesn't make any sense. Is it a trick? The date here is August 31st, 2019. That's yesterday!"

Olivia jerked forward in surprise. "That means this lady, Raven Shadow, came back to the diary and wrote in it yesterday!" Olivia exclaimed.

"Just read it!" Vivian exclaimed, tightening her fists excitedly.

Dash took a deep breath.

"*Saturday, August 31st, 2019*

Yes, this is still me, Raven Shadow. Now I am 28 years old. I have even more secrets than before. The day never did come when I defeated my mother, Dolores Dark. Now, she has taken the name Agnes Howler. She's really powerful, and I could never tell her what I am about to tell you, dearest diary. I am not fond of my mother's bad ways. She's really mean to everyone, especially children. I'm a kind witch, but there's no way I can reveal that to anyone. I wish I were a lot nicer than I am. Sometimes, I do admire my mother, but very, very rarely. I can't believe she turned out to be so greedy for power. I remember her as a strong witch, always ready to do anything to protect her family when I was little. But now, she is happy to hurt people and she does it for fun. Now, she's after four children who seem to have what it takes to defeat the Black Death. I haven't seen that in a while. I hope they succeed and defeat all of us, including me.

Oh, and about Magma! He's still alive. But he's quite a bit larger now. He guards our caves, keeping us safe. I'm so proud of him, but he seems to have taken evil ways from my mother too. Is everyone against me? I built a tunnel leading from the Looming Cliff to my cave. I know it's dangerous, but it's very well hidden. I hope one day it will be useful. There's another one leading to Agnes's house. I feel bad for any unlucky person who chooses to take their path that way."

Dash stopped reading here. "That was her?" he asked. "Wow! I'm glad we didn't take the other tunnel. That wouldn't have been pleasant."

Olivia nodded in agreement. *That wouldn't end well for us!* she thought thankfully.

"So, we're in the house of Agnes's daughter," Olivia said. "Scary." She shuddered.

"The four children she said who have what it takes to defeat the Black Death.'" Vivian remembered what the diary had said. "That's us."

Olivia nodded. "For sure," she said.

Dash closed the diary. "This lady is obviously nice,"

he said, putting the wrinkled book back in the old chest.

"Maybe she can help us," Vivian said, closing the lid of the chest.

Olivia nodded. "But we need to look for disguises right now. We don't know when Raven Shadow will return home."

PowerSurge jumped up and continued their search. They found a bedroom. Olivia looked for any unusual features. There was a black bed with white comforters, held up with tall bedposts with large pointed tops. There was a grey fur rug laid out across the entire floor. The bed looked so soft that Olivia just wanted to take a nap on it. There were two identical black nightstands on each side of the bed. Two closed doors were facing one side of the wall, undoubtedly leading to the bathroom and closet.

Olivia led her friends into the walk-in closet. Ten cloaks hung around her, making her feel like she was trapped in a nightmare. Many canes were hanging on hooks in front of her, all a bright green color. She took one cloak off the rack. It smelled disgusting, almost like the smelly concoction she had seen Agatha drinking.

"This place gives me a weird feeling," Vivian said, shivering. "I want to get out of here now!"

We can't get out now! Olivia thought. *We have a*

mission to accomplish!

"But we need disguises first!" Olivia exclaimed. "Then we can leave to look for Charles! But not yet!"

Vivian nodded. "Hey guys," Vivian called. "Try these on!"

Olivia and Dash rushed over to put on black cloaks.

Dash threw one over his head, attempting to put it on as fast as he possibly could. "It's way too small," he whined.

Olivia laughed. "That's probably because you're wearing it upside-down," she said.

Vivian smiled and put her cloak on. It easily slid over her head and draped down past her feet, spreading across the tiled floor.

"This is way too big," Vivian said.

"I agree," Olivia said, walking over to the cloaks. She saw one that was about her size. She took it off the hanger and handed it to Vivian. "Try this one on," she said.

Vivian slipped the cloak over her head and it fit exactly. "Perfect," she said.

Olivia turned around to see how Dash was getting along. To her surprise, he was not where she last saw him, but was standing in front of the large free-standing mirror. He was jumping around and making different faces.

"Dash!" Olivia exclaimed. "You can't goof off here! We have to find a disguise for you before we get out of here!"

Dash walked back over to her and tried on the cloak properly. "Yeah, it's good," he told her without even looking at it.

Olivia sighed. "Do you guys think these clothes can make us turn into bad people?" she asked worriedly.

"I doubt it," Dash said. "Because Raven has these clothes in her closet, so she wears them. But she's still a good witch. As far as we know."

Olivia nodded. *That sounds reasonable,* she thought. *I really hope Dash is right.*

"We should probably get hats," Vivian said, as she tied the band around the cloak.

"Good idea," Olivia pointed to the witch's hats that were stacked up in the corner of the room. "Let's put them on."

She handed one to each of her friends and put one on herself. As the stiff hat touched her head, she felt an odd sensation pass through her body, as if she was being a bad person for doing what she was doing.

"I feel like a witch," Dash shuddered.

"Me too," Olivia said. "Honestly, this reminds me of my Halloween costume when I was five."

Vivian and Dash chuckled. All of a sudden, Vivan's

face became stone cold.

"You know, we never thought that Raven might've left her 'diary' in the front of her house to trick people that she was good. After all, it wasn't very well hidden."

Before Olivia had time to think, her body stiffened in surprise.

A noise came from the entrance of the house. The sound of keys clinking together filled Olivia's ears. She listened carefully for more noises.

"What was that?" Vivian asked.

Dash shrugged. "We should probably hide," he said.

Olivia wondered how he always stayed so calm. But then, she remembered something. "Guys, she's a good witch, remember?" she said. "Maybe she'll help us!"

Her friends nodded.

"Of course!" Vivian exclaimed.

The sound of a door opening reached Olivia, and she still felt a little bit nervous. *Uh oh! That's probably Raven!* Olivia thought. *How is she going to react? Whether she's good or bad, how would someone like three kids breaking into her house-and reading her private diary!*

"She's coming," Dash warned.

Raven Shadow was opening the door to her bedroom, probably coming home after a visit to the supermarket.

Olivia stepped out of the closet. "Hi!" she exclaimed.

Raven Shadow was so shocked that she almost fell over. She had a young-looking face that was filled with surprise, and her wrinkly hands immediately crossed over her chest. Her skin was pale white. It reminded Olivia of the evil color of Ms. B.'s skin. Raven's skinny nose was pointed toward Olivia. She was wearing the exact same thing as Olivia, but she looked a lot more normal in it. Her green eyes were narrowed.

"And what are three kids doing in my house?" she asked suspiciously.

21

I thought she knew who we were! Olivia thought. *She even wrote about us in her diary!*

Dash stepped forward to answer Raven's question. "We're the four kids you wrote about in your diary," he said. "You know, the ones who are here to save the world? You guessed it, we're important!"

Oh no! Olivia thought. *Why did he tell her that? Now she knows we read her private diary! And we definitely weren't supposed to. And* why *is he talking to her like that? Not a good idea!*

"Well, at least three of them," Dash continued.

Raven looked enraged, and she clenched her fists. PowerSurge still didn't know if Raven was good or not, so Olivia was quite intimidated by Raven's incredibly angry looks.

"So let me get this straight." Raven narrowed her eyes. "You kids broke into my house, read my diary, and now you're playing with my clothes. This isn't a game of dress-up you know."

Olivia suddenly felt stupid standing in witches' clothes.

"Well…basically, yeah," Vivian said. "We're really sorry for doing it. But we needed to. We're looking for some help to defeat your mother."

"So you're on my side then," Raven said skeptically.

Olivia wasn't sure if Raven was willing to trust them completely.

"Oh, and do not call that Agnes lady my mother," Raven said. "That was a long time ago. She has changed so much since then." Thinking about her biological mother made her scowl as she walked over to sit on her cozy bed. "Anyway, what might I help you with?"

Olivia instantly felt relieved after hearing this; now she knew that Raven was a nice woman who was willing to help them. "You see, Ms. Shadow," Olivia began. "We…."

"Call me Raven," Raven interrupted.

Olivia felt odd talking to a full-grown woman as if she were just a child. After all, Raven *was* a witch. She could hurt them if she wanted to.

"Okay, Raven," Olivia said. "We need to find a safe way around the city. We're looking for our friend, the fourth person in our group, PowerSurge. We're trying to defeat Agnes Howler because she is after my dad for the Mystic Pearl. She seems to be possessing him and forcing him to hand it over. We don't know how much longer he'll hold out."

Raven nodded, slowly processing all of the information Olivia had just told her. Suddenly, her eyes widened. She looked at Olivia. It looked like she wanted to do something, but she was holding back.

"You mean, you're my...." Raven started to say.

Olivia frowned. "Your...?" She tried to continue for her.

Raven shook her head. "I have a question. Did your mother disappear when you were born?" she said.

"Wow, you're good at mind reading!" Olivia exclaimed. "Yeah, she did!"

Raven nodded. "So that means you *are* my...." She tried again to say.

"Your what?" Olivia asked, really confused at this point.

"Nothing, it's nothing," Raven said, shaking her head.

Olivia shrugged.

"So you want to disguise yourself as witches in order to sneak around the city?" Raven asked casually as if nothing had happened.

"That'd be us," Dash said. "What, not the best idea?"

Raven smiled. "It's a good idea," she said. "But it would never work in our world."

Of course. The witches had such strong powers; they would be sure to see through a disguise like that. This lady really is *nice,* Olivia thought. *It's like she doesn't even care we broke into her house!*

"So what should we do?" Vivian asked.

Raven motioned to them with her hand. "Come here, young ones," she answered, signaling for them to sit on her soft rug. "Let me tell you a story."

Olivia felt the rug cushion her as she sank into it. It felt good to finally sit down after all they had done.

"What type of story?" Dash asked as he sat down.

Raven smiled. "Just listen," she said. "Once upon a time, there was an ordinary girl, around your age. Strange things always happened around her. Items would randomly shift places, or people would just stop moving, sometimes get hurt for no explainable reason at all. She had a gorgeous mother; her long brown hair and deep blue eyes were just a small portion of her beauty. The young girl wanted to be just like her stunning mother. She wanted to be like the kind, loving soul she thought her mother was—but she was very wrong. One day, her mother told her that she was a witch, just like the rest of her family. At first, the young girl was excited, but that soon changed. It transformed her life completely. She could no longer have friends, and her mother forced her to drop out of school to study witchcraft. All of her training had to be done in secret, and her world soon turned dark. She had nobody to confide in, or share her worries with. Worst of all, nobody was by her side. This girl loved to talk, and she had many friends at school, but they all had to be removed from her now secretive life." Raven paused. Her eyes were tearing up.

"That's so sad," Olivia said.

Raven shifted her position, grabbing a black, lace pillow from behind her.

What's going to happen now? Olivia thought. *And why is Raven even telling us this?*

"One day, her mother came home with a satisfied grin on her face. She told the girl that she had just cast a genius spell on a man, enchanting him to fall in love with her. He would never come out of this love trance until after their second child was born. The girl deeply disagreed with this. She believed that love should be real and true, and that the witches had an advantage if they were able to do this. But her mother didn't listen. She accused the girl of trying to remove her accomplishment. Her mother went on with her daily life, spending more and more time with that man every day. When the girl turned eighteen, she got her degree in witchcraft and was now able to perform any spell she desired considering the Able Witches Law. The girl had grown up to love witchcraft and was ecstatic about this. But she wanted to be a nice witch, generous to the blossoming world around her. However, if her mother found out about this, the girl would be banished from the Witches' World and the few people she loved. Possibly even killed." A small tear started flowing down Raven's face.

Olivia leaned forward to give her a hug.

"It's okay!" Vivian tried to comfort her.

Raven shook her head and kept going with a wet face. "The girl soon found a man she loved. She had never grown up around boys, but she instantly had a feeling that he was the one for her. But when her mother found out about the quickly blossoming love between them, she killed the man with a flick of her magical cane."

PowerSurge gasped. That witch had *killed* someone. Now it really sunk in for Olivia. At that moment, she realized that it meant to take away someone's life. They would never have a second chance. She shook her head and turned her attention back to Raven, determined not to think about death.

"For years, the girl despised her mother for this. She lost her voice countless times from yelling at her mother, and never really forgave her. The man had been completely innocent. But the girl was 18, and soon she had other things to worry about. One day, her mother returned home as usual, but she looked extremely different. Her sparkling crystal-blue eyes had become black, and her gorgeous physique and beautiful hair was covered by a jet-black cape. The mother the girl had once looked up to was now ugly—inside and out. Her mother had just given birth to another child with the man she had cast a love spell on. Apparently, part of the spell was that she herself would turn ugly once the second child was born, but she didn't seem to care about that. About two years passed. The girl became enraged when she realized that her mother had been holding her first child, the boy, captive since his birth to gain possession of something from the man she loved. The girl felt horrible that her mother was holding a child captive, so she tried and tried to convince her mother to let him go. But she just wouldn't budge. The girl loved the toddler like her own. She realized that she had to be his mother figure because an evil witch was his biological mother. She taught him how to read, write, and other things he would have learned at school. But most importantly, she taught him how to recognize the good in the world. The boy's father had gotten the pearl as part of the deal; the girl's mother thought she would be able to get it back easily, but it turned out to be harder than she thought. The girl wanted to kill her mother, to punish her for everything she had done to everyone in her life. But she couldn't. Her mother was too powerful for her, and she had many witches who would back her up if a fight started to brew. The girl had been raised in a dark environment. That's why she wanted to bc the good witch she is today. The girl grew up to be me." At this point, tears were meandering down Raven's face. She wanted to heal her past and move on with the present.

"That was beautiful, but sad at the same time," Dash said.

No wonder she's a kind witch now, Olivia thought. *She knows what it means to really suffer.* "What can we do to help you?" Olivia asked kindly.

"Nothing, little generous one," Raven said, wiping her face with her cloak. "The question is, what can I do for you?"

Olivia shared a glance with Vivian. After such a sad story, it didn't feel right to ask anything from this depressed woman. But they needed to. She was their only hope of finding Charles.

"We need to find a way to travel through the city without being caught," Vivian said.

Raven's face lit up. "We should sneak into Agnes's house! She has a control room where you can see everywhere in this world!" Raven said.

Olivia looked at Dash. *Everywhere?* Olivia thought. *That sure is a lot of power for one person!* "That's a great idea!" Olivia exclaimed. "But how are we going to get inside?"

Raven looked thoughtful. "I could take you on my cane," she said. "I have a very large pot that I can attach to it. You guys can sit in there."

"I think that would work." Vivian grinned. "We should try it. But one quick question, how strong is this pot of yours?"

Raven smiled. "It's strong enough." She stood up and walked into her closet. Seconds later, she emerged with a large cauldron. It was jet black, just like a normal cauldron. Two handles were attached to the sides. "This will have to do. It looks more normal than a bag." Raven opened the drawer of her nightstand and took out some thick string. She tied it tightly to the cauldron and motioned for the children to get inside.

Olivia sat down in the cauldron. It was almost as wide as her dining table. She felt uncomfortable that she couldn't see outside of the pot, and couldn't keep track of what was happening around them. Vivian and Dash settled down beside her in a circle inside the cauldron. They gripped the insides of the cauldron with all their might. PowerSurge had never been on a ride like this before.

"This is big!" Dash's voice echoed across the large pot.

Olivia nodded in agreement. She realized that Dash couldn't see her because it was so dark.

Raven's voice floated into the pot.

"Ready?" she asked.

"We're ready!" Olivia called up to Raven.

Olivia felt the cauldron slowly lift off the floor. Raven took them outside her house. Olivia had no idea how high up they were, but as the wind rushed past the cauldron and Olivia felt the humid air from River Magmus and the volcano, she figured out that they must be quite high. *This is scary,* Olivia thought. *Is this how blind people feel?* She wished once more that she could see outside—especially when the cauldron stopped in midair.

"Greetings," Raven's voice said to someone.

Olivia hoped that the other person couldn't see past the protective blanket covering the cauldron. Raven would be in even more trouble than PowerSurge.

"What are you up to?" sneered the other voice.

22

Olivia shuddered at the sound of the voice. She knew it wasn't Agnes Howler or Agatha Black, but it still scared her. The sound pierced her body. She crumpled up in a ball, hoping she would be invisible to the outsider. Vivian and Dash shifted their positions, causing the cauldron to shake while suspended in midair.

"That would be none of your business, Cassandra," Raven said coldly.

This Cassandra lady sounds scary, Olivia thought. *And powerful.*

"I would ask what was in the pot, but I already know." Cassandra gave a stinging response.

Olivia's body tensed. *How did she know? What will happen now?*

It bothered Olivia that the witches were having a conversation while she and her friends were suspended in midair. *Oh!* Olivia thought. *Cassandra must be using reverse psychology. She's trying to make Raven believe she knows we're here so Raven will reveal what is really inside the cauldron!*

"I never trusted you, Raven," Cassandra sneered. "I know exactly what you're hiding."

"Liar!" Raven sneered. "Next time, keep your puny words to yourself."

Olivia felt Raven speed past Cassandra, not staying to hear her burning retort. Then Olivia and her friends were thrown up in the air in surprise as the bottom of the cauldron collided with the ground.

"Raven," Olivia whispered, still recovering from the landing. "Who was that?"

Raven lifted the blanket off of the cauldron. Olivia squinted as bright sunlight filled the dark cauldron.

"That was Cassandra Crow," Raven growled. "How can such rudeness fit in one body?"

Dash widened his eyes. "Did she really know we were here?" he asked nervously.

Raven shook her head. "I doubt it," she said. "But we'd better get going, just in case."

The blanket covered the top of the cauldron, shielding them from the wandering eyes outside. *Back to darkness again,* Olivia thought, *I'm tired of only being able to see black.*

"I wonder what will happen when we reach Agnes's house," Vivian said.

They lifted off again, reaching top height. They zoomed towards Agnes's house at a very high speed. Olivia was thrown forward as Raven started descending very fast. Olivia felt like throwing up when she felt dizzy. She lurched forward. Then she and her friends thumped onto the ground as the cauldron landed on a hard surface.

"We're here!" Raven exclaimed, lifting the blanket off of the cauldron.

Olivia stood up, stretching her legs. She was in a valley that had no plants at all. It was humongous, the size of ten football fields put together. It was the dark color of burned lava that had hardened into rock. Dips in the ground made it look almost like the back of a snake. Beyond the large valley, Olivia saw a house—fancier and greater than any she could ever dream of. It was constructed out of white marble—and, in Olivia's opinion, was the only color in Witches' World worth looking at. The roof was shaped like the dorsal fins of sharks, all made of shiny glass. The building reminded her of the Sydney Opera house, but grander. A magnificent double-door was in the middle of the exterior wall. Its outline of black obsidian greatly contrasted the main color of the house. Golden bars marked the door handles. Tall, white pillars stood in front of the house, seeming to hold up the flawless roof. *This must be the building I saw from up on Looming Cliff,* Olivia thought.

That could only mean one thing; this was the house of Agnes Howler.

23

"Follow me," said Raven. "We have to get out of here soon. There's going to be a meeting in an hour. They're always held at Agnes's house."

Olivia hurriedly followed Raven across the charred field, hoping an hour would be enough time to save Charles and defeat the witches. *How did the witches even build this place?* Olivia thought. *Probably magic.*

"How many witches are in the Black Death?" Dash asked as he stuffed his hands in his pockets.

"Exactly forty including Agnes and me," said Raven. "But a lot of them are just trainees. Only fourteen of us will be attending the meeting. We are the only certified witches according to the Able Witches Law."

Olivia suddenly remembered something she had heard when PowerSurge was in Agatha Black's office in the escape room.

"Wait a sec, shouldn't you be calling her Master Agnes?" Olivia asked.

Raven shook her head. "I really should. But I don't when I'm alone, or not around other witches," she said. "But seriously, who calls their mother 'Master'? No matter how powerful she is, a mother should be addressed as 'Mother' or 'Mom' by her own children."

I wonder how Agnes even qualifies to be a mother, Olivia thought. *She's so un-maternal!*

Olivia agreed with her, but she thought that it was risky to disobey Agnes's orders, even though she was Raven's mother. Not calling her 'Master' might get Raven in trouble, but helping PowerSurge would probably give Raven consequences that nobody in the Witches' World had ever faced before.

After what felt like years to Olivia, they finally reached the grand front door of Agnes's house.

Raven placed her hand on the golden handle. A beep sound came from the door and it was unlocked.

"That's cool," Dash said.

"This mechanism has been around for years," Raven

said. "If a member of the Black Death touches it, the door unlocks." She opened the door.

"Whoa!" Vivian gasped.

The house was grander than Olivia could ever have imagined. The front door opened into a large living room. Its walls were made of cooled lava rock, so shiny that Olivia could see her astounded reflection in it. A grand fireplace was in the middle of the front wall. A blazing fire heated the humongous room. Couches were spread out around the room, all of cozy red velvet. The main thing Olivia noticed were many pictures on the glistening walls, all lined up as if in a timeline. They all portrayed women in the same clothing that Agnes wore. Olivia realized that they must be the past leaders of the Black Death. Small rectangular pools on the floor were filled with crystal-clear water, adding a touch to the room. Large white tiles, with small dashes of gray, covered the floor. The ceiling was incredibly high; a large crystal chandelier hung from it and was reflected onto the movie-screen sized TV. The sparkling windows made the room seem five times bigger than it actually was. The children's faces demonstrated looks of astonishment. They had never seen such a beautiful mansion; they were amazed at how grand a house could look.

"This place is AWESOME!" Dash exclaimed,

bouncing onto one of the couches.

"Hush!" Raven whispered. "I don't know if someone is home."

Dash immediately stopped jumping around and scuttled to Raven's side.

"Come along." Raven motioned for Olivia, Vivian, and Dash to follow her up a spiral staircase. A plush carpet was laid on top of the sparkling, marble steps. After a few minutes, they entered a large room. About five hundred monitors were displayed across the walls, showing every room in Witches' World.

Olivia stepped forward and ran her fingers across the screen of one of the monitors. She was looking at someone's living room. She felt that this was incredibly intrusive to the privacy of the witches, no matter how evil they were. *I don't think that the other witches are comfortable with Agnes invading their privacy like that!* Olivia thought. *There's a limit to power!*

"Hey! Look!" Dash exclaimed from across the room. "I think that's Charles!"

Olivia hurried toward Dash. On the screen of one of the monitors, she saw a Charles-like figure sitting in a chair. He seemed to be tied to the chair with rope. His back was facing her, so she couldn't see his face. Seeing Charles in that state bothered her. Had the Black Death hurt him? Olivia prayed that he was okay and that they hadn't done anything to him. Some witches were sitting in other chairs, surrounding the hostage. Olivia felt resentment as she looked at their evil faces. *You kidnapped my best friend!* she thought fiercely. *You will pay, and we will make it happen!*

"That's definitely him," Vivian said. "He's wearing the same clothes as he was before."

Olivia nodded. "That's him," she told Raven.

Raven leaned forward and looked at the features of the room. "Oh no!" she exclaimed.

Olivia anxiously traded glances with her friends. "What?" Olivia asked nervously. She silently sent a prayer to her grandpa in the hope that they could find Charles, defeat the Black Death, and easily leave Witches' World.

"That is the meeting room of the witches," Raven said, shaking her head. "In forty-five minutes, the meeting will start. You can see some of them are already there."

Olivia's body grew cold. They had to find a way to rescue Charles. "We have to make a plan," Olivia said, determined to succeed.

But Raven looked down sadly. "I'm sorry, dear," she said. "But it's impossible."

24

That can't be true! Olivia thought. *Not after all this!* They had been through too much hard work just to hear that it would be impossible to succeed. No. Olivia just wouldn't accept it. "There has to be a way," she said. "We'll find one. We're not leaving without Charles."

Raven stepped away from the children. "I have to go to the meeting now. They will suspect something if I do not get there soon," she said. "It's up to you children now. I cannot do more for you. I hope you rescue your friend and defeat Agnes. Really, I do." She turned and walked out of the room without looking back.

Olivia didn't like how Raven gave up so easily.

Olivia watched the monitor showing the room Charles was in. A minute later, she saw Raven take a seat in one of the chairs.

Raven looked up at the camera. Knowing Olivia would be watching, she mouthed, 'I'm sorry.'

Olivia turned to look at her friends.

"We have to find a way," Vivian said, determined to save the life of her cousin.

Dash nodded in agreement. He sat in one of the chairs. "Actually, I have an idea," he said. "You see, the witches seem to listen to everything Agnes says. What if we faked a command from her? She's not in the room, so it could work."

Olivia went through his plan in her head before she answered. "It definitely could work," she said. "But what would we say?"

Vivian stood up and started pacing around the room. "We have to say something to make them get out of the room," she said. "How about if we pretend that Agnes screams for them?"

"Great!" Olivia exclaimed. "Vivian, you pretend to scream for help. Dash and I will be hiding in the meeting room. I watched Raven walk up the stairs, so it has to be upstairs. Then we'll rescue Charles and meet you back here." It seemed like it would work.

"Sounds good," Dash said. "Let's go!"

Olivia followed Dash up another flight of posh stairs, keeping a lookout for witches and reducing their sounds so nobody would hear them.

When Olivia heard the sounds of people talking, she assumed that it was the witches' meeting room. *Here,* she signaled to Dash. She peeked around the corner. Her heart skipped a beat as she saw ten witches sitting in armchairs beside one another in a circle. They were all almost as skinny and bony as Ms. B. They were also quite tall, making it scarier to look at them. The witches were dressed in black cloaks and pointy hats. More witches were entering from the entrance opposite to where Olivia and Dash stood. Charles was sitting in the middle of the circle, looking more helpless in real life than on video. *Hold on Charles,* Olivia thought. *We'll save you soon!*

"Hello, Esme," a cool voice sounded from inside the room. "Welcome."

A stunning witch took a seat with her back to Olivia and Dash.

"Pleasant to see you, Nyx," Esme said darkly.

Why are these witches so formal with each other? Olivia thought. *After all, they're all bad.* She noticed that now there was only one empty chair in the circle; it was obviously awaiting the leader of the Black Death. It was a lot taller than the others and was on a raised platform. Agatha Black proudly sat in one of the armchairs with her legs crossed and her bony arms on the armrests. Olivia viewed her with hateful disgust.

"Ah, Esme," Agatha said. "I hear your potion proved successful."

Seeing Agatha reminded Olivia of who got PowerSurge in this mess in the first place. After the mission, Olivia never ever wanted to think about Agatha ever again.

"Oh yes," Esme said. "You just needed the right amount of blood and teeth."

Olivia shuddered.

"They're all there except for Agnes," Olivia whispered to Dash who was behind her. All of a sudden, Olivia heard a deafening scream from below.

"HELP!" the voice yowled.

At first, Olivia thought that it was Agnes, but then she recognized something familiar in Vivian's voice.

The witches in the room looked at each other nervously, as if they were daring the others to see what had happened. Some of them didn't know whether to believe the cry, but they knew that if they didn't check, they might get in huge trouble. All of a sudden, Charles jerked his head up.

Did he recognize Vivian's voice? Olivia wondered. *Would he help them?*

Charles made as many noises as he could, considering a piece of tape covered his mouth.

Esme stood up and ripped it off. "What?" she snarled.

"Don't go," Charles said.

What? Olivia thought. *Have they hypnotized Charles also? Why does it seem like he is working against us?*

"It's probably just a trap," Charles said. "Trust me."

Esme laughed. "And why exactly should we trust a hostage?" she snickered.

"Fine then, don't trust me," Charles said. "But you'll regret it."

The witches shared glances.

"Maybe he's trying to trick us," Nyx said. "Maybe we should go."

Agatha frowned. "I don't know. He is a pretty smart kid," she said. "He could be trying to make us go so he can escape."

"Oh come on, Agatha," another witch laughed. "How in the world is he going to escape? I say we go."

"Me too. We could get in trouble with Master Agnes if she really is hurt," Nyx said. She stood up and left the room, with others following her. At this point, half of the witches were hurriedly exiting the room to check on Agnes.

Olivia knew that wasn't enough. "It's not working," she whispered anxiously.

Dash closed his eyes with worry.

One witch fidgeted in her chair as if debating whether she should leave or not.

Please leave, Olivia thought. She willed Vivian to keep going to cause the other witches to leave.

"NOW!" the voice yelled. "OR ELSE YOU WILL FACE THE CONSEQUENCES!"

The rest of the witches left. All except one. Finally, she pointed her finger, glared at Charles, and left. The room was empty except for poor Charles.

Olivia and Dash rushed inside the room and hurried to Charles's side. It seemed like the witches had treated him well so far, as they didn't know what they would do with him.

"Charles!" Olivia whispered. "Come with us!"

Charles was smiling. It was pretty obvious to Olivia that he knew what was going on.

"I knew you would come," he said. "I was trying to help you. Now, can you please get me out of these stupid ropes?"

Olivia smiled as she and Dash unknotted the ropes as fast as they possibly could.

Suddenly, Charles's eyes widened. He pointed to something behind Olivia. She turned around.

It was Raven.

"You did it!" she said. "You children are so smart!"

Charles didn't know that Raven was on their side. He immediately jumped to the conclusion that they had been caught.

"Relax," Olivia told Charles. "She's a good witch. She helped us out a lot. We'll tell you all about it later."

Olivia and Dash were almost done untangling Charles when Vivian hurtled into the room.

"Jump off the balcony!" she panted. "Now! They're after us!"

Olivia untied Charles's last knot and ran to the balcony.

Raven fled from the crime scene to cover all of their footprints.

"But we'll fall and probably die!" Charles said, breathing heavily.

Olivia leaned over the balcony railing. "There's one below!" she said. "Aim for that!"

As Olivia jumped off of the large balcony, she heard Raven call, "Good luck, children!"

Thankfully, she and her friends landed on the one below. Olivia's back ached from the fall. Her friends lay on their backs beside her. Looking up, she saw something towering over her. She then realized that she was in the one situation that she had never, ever, *ever* wanted to be in.

"Well, well, well!" a voice sneered.

It was Agnes.

25

"Not now," Olivia muttered fearfully. *Please, we were so close!* she thought. Agnes was the last challenge she needed to face before leaving the Witches' World.

"Now is the perfect time," Agnes growled. "You're not getting past me again!"

Suddenly, Olivia felt the ground tremble. She looked around. What could that be? It happened again. Olivia turned and saw what caused the vibrations. It was Volcano Magmus. She saw smoke streaming out of its peak. It was about to erupt, destroying everything in its path, including Olivia and her friends. *It's going to be absolutely destructive!* Olivia thought. *This world is probably going to be blown apart when it erupts!*

"The volcano," Vivian whispered in Olivia's ear.

Olivia nodded, barely moving her head. She kicked Charles's leg, motioning for him and Dash to look behind them.

"What do you want from us now?" Olivia asked. She wasn't going to show Agnes that she was scared.

"Oh, just everything I have always wanted," Agnes sneered. "The Mystic Pearl, my justice—but most of all, I want you kids dead like a potato crisp on a Sunday afternoon."

Olivia frowned. Agnes had no clue what she was talking about.

"Well, you're not getting it," Charles retorted.

Agnes looked at him, for once taking her evil eyes off Olivia. "You escaped!" she growled.

"I have friends," Charles said, shrugging his shoulders.

The ground trembled again, more violently than the last time.

"The watch," Dash whispered. "Where is it?"

Olivia's heart skipped a beat. They needed the watch to escape the Witches' World! If Dash didn't have it, then where was it? Olivia suddenly remembered that they had left it in the woods, forgetting all about it as they jumped in the lake.

Dash had spoken too loudly. A large grin formed on Agnes's face.

"Oh, cane, my cane," she enchanted as she closed her eyes. "Bring me the watch now!"

Out of nowhere, Charles's watch came flying towards Agnes at such a high speed that Olivia had to duck to avoid having her head chopped off.

"Agnes, one question," Olivia tried to talk as if Agnes was just a random person, in order to hide her fear. "If you know such strong magic, then why couldn't you just force the pearl out of my dad's hands and leave us all alone?"

"Because the pearl is not the only thing I want from him," Agnes said, grinning. "I want your father too, Olivia."

Olivia traded a glance with her friends.

"What do you mean?" Olivia asked curiously.

"Silly child," Agnes sneered. She looked right at Olivia.

Olivia saw some warmth shift into Agnes's eyes. But it only lasted for a few seconds.

Then Agnes spoke the words that Olivia never imagined could come from her mouth. She didn't have any time to think before she heard the shock of her life.

"Olivia...I am your mother."

26

"Liar," Olivia spluttered. *How is that possible?* she thought. *No! I just won't accept it!* But she knew it was true. Piecing together all of the parts, it made sense. Agnes had cast a love spell on Olivia's dad, causing him to have kids with her. After Olivia was born, her dad stopped loving Agnes, just like the spell had asked. Agnes had become ugly after that. But somehow, Olivia's dad had kept the Mystic Pearl, greatly enraging Agnes. So Agnes stole his son in order to get it back. But he wouldn't budge for eight years, so she stole Vivian's brother. Still, no result. So Agnes decided to start controlling his mind, every minute driving him crazy, pulling him closer to handing over the Mystic

Pearl. He was holding up—until now. Olivia realized that Agnes would soon be the proud controller of Olivia, her family, the Mystic Pearl, and all of Olivia's friends. But that would only happen if Agnes survived, and there was no way that PowerSurge was going to let that happen. Their biggest ally would be the volcano and the lava river, bubbling, ready to kill anybody. But how could Olivia communicate with her friends when Agnes was standing right over her, keeping track of any move Olivia made? *That must be why stupid Agnes knows so much about my family!* Olivia thought in disgust. *How did I not realize this before?* She knew that this meant she was half-witch, but she would never do anything about it. If she had powers, she would leave them be. Agnes was possessed—and in a bad way. Olivia never wanted to turn out like her, even if that meant ignoring the special abilities she had. And no matter what their genetic bond, Agnes would never be Olivia's mother in her mind.

"Whether you like it or not, it's true." Agnes snickered.

Why couldn't someone kind like Raven be my mother instead? A thought rushed into Olivia's mind. *Does this make Raven my sister? But that wasn't possible. Raven is so much older than me.*

"No, it's not." Dash defended Olivia. "We have no reason to believe you after everything you've done."

"Yeah," Charles said. "You're just a stupid witch with silly powers. Stop trying to manipulate us into doing what you want us to do."

"Charles and Dash are right," Vivian said. "Plus, Olivia is *way* too nice to have a cruel mother like you."

"That's what you want to believe," Agnes said with a sinister smile. She obviously enjoyed the attention. "But you have to know that I am telling you the truth. Like it or not. I like it. I need the Mystic Pearl, and *you* will help me get it."

"So, is Raven my sister?" Olivia asked.

Agnes seemed confused about how Olivia knew Raven was her daughter. Then Agnes seemed to realize that Raven had helped PowerSurge.

Olivia instantly regretted what she had said.

"Tell me, children," Agnes spoke slowly with a fake smile on her face. "Did Raven help you with your mission?"

Olivia didn't want to give away Raven's cover. She waited for her friends to answer. *Agnes mustn't know!* Olivia thought. *That would be the end of Raven!*

"No," Vivian murmured, lying to protect the only hint of good in the cruel Black Death.

"She did, didn't she?" Agnes shook her head. She

obviously didn't believe Vivian. Agnes's mouth changed into a furious smile.

Olivia's heart stopped cold. She couldn't mistake the look in Agnes's eyes. They portrayed a look so angry that they looked like they were about to burst.

"I NEVER TRUSTED HER!" Agnes roared with all her might.

Olivia felt the ground tremble. This time, she wasn't sure if it was the volcano or if it was Agnes's protruding, loud voice.

"RAVEN! GET OVER HERE! NOW!" Agnes stormed into the meeting room, pulling the children behind her.

Raven was sitting in one of the armchairs, her body trembling as she heard her mother yell her name.

"Y-y-yes," Raven said. She traded a look with Olivia, seeming to realize that her cover was blown.

Olivia mouthed the word, 'sorry.' Raven looked away.

"COME HERE, RIGHT NOW!" Agnes growled.

Raven shakily stood up and helplessly walked towards her cruel mother. "Yes, Lo-Lord," she murmured.

Olivia felt so much pity building up in her heart as she watched the generous woman succumb to her mother.

"DID YOU HELP THESE CHILDREN TRY TO DEFEAT YOUR OWN MOTHER?" Agnes roared.

Raven nodded her head ever so slowly as if she knew that Agnes was going to punish her, no matter what her answer was.

Agnes pointed her cane at Raven. "OH CANE, MY CANE," she cried, with no gentleness whatsoever in her tone. "KILL THIS WOMAN ONCE AND FOR ALL!"

Raven tossed and turned, desperately trying to survive the spell. "Please!" she screamed in agony as she trembled on the floor.

Olivia sucked in her breath as she watched in pain, then turned her attention to Agnes who had a huge grin on her face as she enjoyed the torture happening in front of her.

The whole room went still as a final wave of anguish rippled through Raven's body.

Olivia's world seemed to stop as she stared at Raven's lifeless body, lying in the middle of the witches' meeting room, and Agnes smiling over it with a look of satisfaction on her face.

27

Why couldn't I have sacrificed myself for Raven? Why did Raven have to die? Olivia thought as immense hate for Agnes rushed through her body, making her more determined than ever before. Another huge tremor shook the ground, returning her grieving mind to the present. *I can't feel bad for the past,* she thought. *We must defeat the Black Death for Raven's sake, or I'll never forgive myself.*

"So, let's start this meeting." Agnes ambled to her chair, pausing to kick Raven's body.

Olivia vowed that she and her friends would defeat Agnes if it was the last thing they did. They needed to start by finding the Mystic Pearl. Suddenly, Olivia realized that the volcano would erupt soon, destroying everything in its path—including the witches. That is if PowerSurge could stop the witches from leaving their world. A plan rushed into Olivia's mind. She needed to communicate with her friends. The ground shook again.

"Oh Lord, the volcano!" exclaimed a witch on the far side of the room. The witches started to file back in after realizing that Vivian's call was a decoy.

As Agnes looked out the window, she realized that the volcano was going to erupt and destroy her home. "Oh, don't worry, Luna," she said. "We have an hour or so. I can tell by the sound of the trembling."

The witch nodded and relaxed back into her chair.

"The children," one of the witches said. "What will we do with them?"

"Zelda and Esther, lock them up somewhere," Agnes demanded.

Two witches nodded and stood up. They escorted PowerSurge upstairs and into a dark prison room, lit with only three candles.

"Now, don't get any ideas," one of the witches warned.

Olivia looked around the dark room, shivering.

"Vivian, is that you?" a voice said.

"MAX!" Vivian exclaimed, running towards her

long-lost brother. She enveloped him in such a huge hug that Max almost toppled over. Max looked pretty much the same, just like Vivian. His brown eyes were a replica of hers and his usually straight hair was uncombed. He was wearing a baseball T-shirt and jeans and bright red shoes. Olivia guessed that the witches had been supplying the prisoners with the bare essentials of fresh clothes, food, and water; and had been cutting their hair.

"How did you find us?" Max asked, hugging Vivian back.

"It's a long story," Olivia sighed. Then she realized Max had said 'us.' "Who do you mean by us?" she asked.

Max stepped to one side, revealing another boy. "This is Jayden," he gestured to the boy. "Olivia's brother."

Olivia looked at her brother and realized how much he looked like her dad. He was a little bit taller than Max. Olivia could just make out sloppy hair, exactly the same light brown color as hers. His brown eyes also looked like hers. He was wearing a baggy sweatshirt and a red baseball cap. But what made him look like her dad was his smile. She could barely see him in the dark, but his smile stood out beautifully. It seemed real and true, not like Agnes's fake smiles. Olivia instantly felt a bond between them.

"Hello, Olivia," he said. His voice was comforting. "I am Jayden, your brother."

My brother? The words rang in Olivia's head. *My brother! Can my family get any more complicated?* She stepped forward and gave him a hug. She had never met him before, and it felt weird to give him a hug. But he was her brother, and they obviously had a close blood relationship. As he hugged her back, she could picture her grandpa and Raven, side by side, smiling as they watched this moment come to life.

"So, what led you to us?" Max asked.

"Witches! Kidnapping! Science teachers! Volcanoes! Mystic Pearl! WE HAVE TO GET OUT OF HERE!" Dash yelled, letting out a huge breath when he finished.

"Whoa, whoa, whoa." Jayden calmed Dash down. "You probably need to repeat that."

"What Dash was probably trying to say is that the volcano will erupt in an hour, so we don't have time to explain now. But we have to find the Mystic Pearl and leave to defeat these witches once and for all," Olivia said.

"But that's what I said!" Dash frowned.

"Not exactly," Olivia said with a smile. "What about you guys?" she asked Jayden and Max

"Well, all I can say is that it feels awesome to see humans other than Max and witches," Jayden said. "I've been locked up in this house all my life."

Olivia felt bad for Jayden. He was already thirteen years old and had missed out on so much being stuck with Agnes all his life. How did he even manage to stay a good person? Who raised him? Suddenly she remembered Raven's story that she must have been the one who taught Jayden everything he knew.

"Olivia, our dad came to visit me up until I was two years old. Then, all of a sudden, he stopped coming. I heard the witches saying that he didn't love Agnes anymore. I don't know why he didn't come back for me, but I never forgot him. A kind witch named Raven Shadow raised me. As soon as we escape, I would like to see her."

Olivia, Charles, Vivian, and Dash looked at each other.

"Listen, Jayden," Charles said. "We're really sorry, there was nothing we could do, please forgive us, we didn't mean...."

"Get to the point, Charles," Jayden said jokingly.

"Raven's dead," Charles said with difficulty.

"W-h-how?" Jayden asked, his smile wiped off his shocked face.

"Agnes," was all Vivian said. Then she turned to

Max. "What about you?"

"I've been stuck here for two years," Max said, putting a hand on Jayden's shoulder. "Thankfully, I met Jayden. It made the stay a lot better, but it definitely wasn't good. We've been here for so long, but we haven't found a way to escape."

"But now we have six heads instead of two," Dash said. "We should be able to find a way. Let's try."

So they stood up to get to work.

Suddenly, a voice that didn't sound like Jayden's came from his mouth.

"All six must unite,
From a high cost,
To defeat evil from left and right,
Or all hope will be lost."

28

Jayden shook his head. The room went silent. *Does he have magical powers or something?* Olivia wondered.

"Jayden, are you okay?" Olivia asked, rushing to his side.

He nodded.

"Sometimes that happens to him. He gets visions, too," Max said to PowerSurge.

Olivia didn't know what that meant, but she knew that Jayden would be important to the mission to defeat the Black Death.

"I think I know what the words meant," Dash said. "All six must mean us. We have to defeat the Black Death or 'all hope will be lost.'"

"That makes sense. So let's find a way out of here," Vivian said.

Another large rumble shook the ground. The six kids, more determined than ever before, once again started to search for ways to escape.

"Hold up a second." Jayden interrupted their work after a few minutes. "This is odd. This door seems to automatically lock. We can unlock it from the inside, if we find the right piece and move it."

"So, do you think we can get out?" Olivia asked her brother.

He squinted through the crack that separated the door from the wall. "I think so," he said, engrossed in his work. "But we're going to need everyone's help. And I need some light."

Dash and Charles picked up the candles and held them by the door.

"Much better," Jayden said. He started looking into the space near the lock.

"Any luck?" asked Max.

"Aha!" Jayden exclaimed. "Look, there's the piece that keeps the door locked. I need the person with the smallest fingers to slide it to the left, so it leaves the space that locks the door. Then, we need to push the door forward as hard as possible, so the piece that juts forward dislodges from the lock and goes outside. After that, we should be able to go."

Vivian stepped forward. "I have small fingers. Maybe I can try?" She placed her fingers in the crack by the door and felt around for the piece Jayden talked about.

It clicked as it slid to the left.

"Nice, Vivian!" Jayden exclaimed. "Now everyone needs to get by the door, and push as hard as they can."

Olivia, Dash, Charles, Jayden, Max, and Vivian each put both hands on the door.

"Push!" Max yelled.

With the whole team's effort, the door moved forward and unlocked, freeing the kids from the dark room and letting them out into the hallway.

"Great job, Jayden!" Olivia exclaimed.

Everyone nodded their heads in definite agreement.

Jayden blushed and looked away.

Another rumble shook the ground, spoiling the happy moment. This one was a lot worse than the last. It seemed like only minutes before the volcano would erupt.

"Out!" A piercing shriek came from the meeting room downstairs. It sounded like Agnes was reacting to the last rumble.

"Guys, it's not safe for us to go through the front door of the house," Olivia said. "We'd have to pass the meeting room, and that's where the witches are."

"For sure, but I know an even better way out," Charles said. "The watch."

"We don't have it anymore," Olivia said. "Agnes does."

"We have to get it back." Dash stated the obvious. "But how?"

29

"Well, where is Agnes right now?" Max said. "If the watch is the only way for us to get out, she probably has it near her."

"Good thinking, Max," Vivian said. "We know she was in the meeting room, but she's probably left it to run away from the volcano."

"I say we check the meeting room," Olivia said. "We have to be careful though." She started down the hallway, careful to tread lightly on the maroon carpet. After heading down the stairs and through another hallway, the children reached the meeting room.

"I can't hear any noise, so there's probably nobody inside," Dash whispered.

Charles poked his head in the room and nodded his head. "All clear," he said, leading the way inside the room.

Another aggressive tremor shook the building. Olivia was almost thrown to the ground.

Olivia desperately looked around the room. The chair that she knew was Agnes's stood out. Its luscious black color was complemented with the green gems that studded the top. The chair was poised majestically on a raised platform. Draped over the armrest, looking like it had been forgotten, was the watch.

"The watch!" Jayden exclaimed, spotting it at the same time as Olivia. He rushed forward and picked it up. "Is this the one you guys were talking about?"

"Yeah, that's it!" Charles exclaimed, running over to take it from Jayden.

"Yes, yes, yes, yes, yes!" Dash yelled. "Now we need to find the Mystic Pearl! But where could it be?"

"I know what I have to do," Olivia said, touching the necklace her grandpa had given her. "I have to call my grandpa." She took a deep breath and removed the necklace. Within seconds, the comforting shape of Olivia's grandpa appeared in front of her. Olivia opened her mouth to speak, but he stopped her.

"Before you ask your question, I need to tell you that I only have a few seconds to speak with you," he said in a rushed but calm tone.

"Hi, Grandpa!" Olivia exclaimed. She knew she didn't have much time, but she still had to greet her elders properly.

"Hello, dear." Her grandpa grinned, enveloping her in a quick, but tight and meaningful hug.

"How are we supposed to defeat the Black Death, Grandpa?" Olivia had to ask even though she didn't know if he would answer her. He obviously seemed like he didn't like giving direct answers to anyone—no matter what.

He merely nodded and conveyed the fact that she would have to figure it out based on what he said. She hoped it would be helpful, and not just a random saying that he had come up with.

"I have one message for you, precious one. It is something I have already told you. Good luck!"

With that, he was gone, before Olivia barely had time to blink.

"Huh," she said, confused. *As if that helped!* Then her common sense and attention returned to her. "How am I supposed to remember?"

"Think, Olivia, think!" Dash exclaimed, shaking her by her shoulders.

Olivia thought as hard as she had ever thought in her ten years of living on the earth.

"I don't know!" she exclaimed, desperate.

"C'mon, Olivia, you can do this!" Vivian exclaimed.

Suddenly, Olivia remembered something her grandpa had told her when he had visited her in her dream. Looking out the window, she saw smoke filling the air. It looked like it was forming words.

"Look for the sign in the smoke," she said. She watched in awe as the words formed before her smart, brown eyes. "There it is—the sign in the smoke."

30

"What does it say?" Max asked, confused.

Olivia concentrated on the words and blocked out her friends' voices. For a second, the smoke spelled out a sentence, instructing Olivia and her friends what they had to do. Olivia read the words out loud.

"*Olivia Mendoza must touch the Mystic Pearl.*"

"Well, where do we find the Mystic Pearl?" Dash asked.

It seemed as if they wouldn't make it. After all, the Mystic Pearl was in the human world. At least, that's what they had assumed.

Then Olivia stood up straight as an idea rushed into her head. "How do we know the Mystic Pearl is at home?" she asked. "My dad could have hidden it here when he came to visit Jayden."

"Of course!" Charles exclaimed. "But where would it be?"

Dash and Olivia shared a glance. There was something that Olivia's dad had always loved: bowling.

"The bowling alley!" Olivia and Dash chorused together.

"Raven let me out to roam around every once in a while. I know where it is! Follow me!" Jayden exclaimed.

They followed Jayden to the bowling alley, running as fast as they could through hallways and up staircases.

"Here it is." Jayden gestured to a room. "The bowling alley."

Olivia looked around at the large room. Three bowling lanes were in a line with couches placed around them. A large bar was in the back of the room. But the main thing that caught Olivia's eyes were the hundreds upon hundreds of balls, racked up on the front wall. As far as she knew, the Mystic Pearl could be the size of a bowling ball.

"How often does Agnes come in here?" Vivian asked Jayden.

Olivia almost fell over as another violent rumble shook the ground. It seemed like the volcano would erupt any minute. A few bowling balls fell off the racks. The place was starting to smell like rotten eggs.

"Never," Jayden said.

"Charles!" Olivia yelled. "Get the watch ready to teleport us!"

Charles took the watch out of his pocket and held it in his hands.

"Do you know how to use it?" Max asked.

"My dad told me how," Charles said.

Another rumble caused more bowling balls to fall off the rack. Olivia's eyes scanned the racks, looking for a ball that was out of the ordinary. But she had no luck. She knew the ball must be hidden somewhere. There was no way it would be out in the open when people would be around it every day. More bowling balls fell off the rack after another violent shake. Now there were only about a hundred balls left on the rack. Olivia and her friends rushed towards the rack, dodging falling balls, but keeping a lookout for the Mystic Pearl. One last shake caused all of the balls to fall off the rack—except for one.

It was so shiny that Olivia had to look away because of the brightness of its surface. It was glowing, lighting up the whole room with the power of only one ball. It looked like something out of Olivia's dream. Something she had never seen before. There was only one thing it could be....

The Mystic Pearl.

31

It's beautiful, Olivia thought. *Absolutely gorgeous.* Its hiding place was genius, as nobody would expect it to be there—even though it was right out in the open. She stared at the Mystic Pearl until another rumble made her fall over. She slowly stood up, off-balance on the shaking ground. The walls of the building were beginning to crack. The Mystic Pearl was on the fourth row, at just the right height for her to reach it.

"Go on." Max encouraged Olivia to touch the Mystic Pearl.

Olivia slowly walked forward, her eyes focused on the shimmering ball. She held out her hand and was millimeters away from touching the ball when Charles's shout caused her to yank back her hand.

"Wait!" Charles yelled. "We all have to hold hands or the watch will only teleport me!" He grabbed Dash's hand because he was standing right next to him. Vivian grabbed hold of Charles's hand and took hold of Jayden's. Jayden grabbed Max's hand. Max slowly took hold of Olivia's hand.

"Go!" Vivian yelled.

I'm scared! Olivia thought. *What if we fail and get stuck here?* She laid her trembling hand on the sleek surface of the Mystic Pearl.

A deafening boom sounded. A flash of light appeared in front of their eyes. The Witches' World blasted apart. Searing heat burnt Olivia's skin right before she and her friends were thrust through an invisible portal, transporting them back into the human world.

"Did we do it?" Olivia asked her friends.

"I think so," Dash said happily.

They were all sprawled across the leaf-covered bank where they had begun their adventure, beside the lake that led them into the Witches' World. But when Olivia looked around, the lake was nowhere to be seen.

"The lake is gone!"

Olivia realized that Max had not let go of her hand yet.

He looked at her as he realized that as well. "Oh, sorry," he apologized, quickly letting go.

Olivia shook her head happily. *It feels so good to be back home,* she thought. *Knowing our mission is accomplished!*

"The witches are defeated, and we are all alive." Olivia smiled. "No need to apologize. I couldn't have asked for a better ending."

Max smiled in agreement.

Olivia heard a scrambling sound and turned to look behind her.

"Olivia!" the voice called.

It was her dad! Olivia stood up and ran towards him, her arms ready for a hug.

"Dad!" she exclaimed, hugging him. "We defeated the Black Death and we found Max and Jayden!"

Her dad looked so proud at that moment, he seemed like he was about to burst. This was the Miguel Mendoza Olivia knew. Since Agnes was dead, her dad wasn't being controlled by her anymore.

"Jayden, is that you?" her dad asked. The familiar shape of Jayden appeared beside Olivia.

"Yes, Dad," Jayden said.

Miguel smiled and hugged Jayden so hard that Jayden made a face at Olivia.

Olivia laughed. Her family was reunited. They were

happier without her evil and cruel mother.

"I haven't seen you in ten years. I'm so sorry I couldn't visit you. Agnes wouldn't let me," Miguel murmured, hugging Jayden again. "Are you alright? You've been with those witches for so many years, I wouldn't be surprised if you learned witchcraft yourself. So tell me, how have you been?"

"It would take a while for us to tell you everything," Jayden said. "Let's go home first."

Miguel motioned for Max, Dash, Charles, and Vivian to come forward. They stood in a line with Olivia and Jayden, with their exhausted eyes focused on Miguel.

"Words cannot express how proud I am of you!" Miguel said. "I have been controlled by Agnes this whole time, ever since PowerSurge started having suspicions about Agatha. Did you wonder what I was doing in the woods? That was all Agnes's fault. She was using my mind to find out about PowerSurge, and what your next move was. You shouldn't have told me everything, because Agnes was hearing it. I stopped being controlled the second you defeated Agnes. Now I can begin to understand what really happened."

Olivia slowly processed her dad's explanation. "Dad, I have so many questions for you," she said. "Is

Raven Shadow actually my sister? Is, or was, Agnes really my mother?"

"Raven was born from a different father," Miguel said. "Agnes put a love potion on me, which made you and Jayden come to life. Which I am glad of because otherwise, you wouldn't be here."

"There's also something I've always wondered," Vivian said. "Why do Charles, Dash, and I all have only one living parent? Is it just a coincidence, or is there a reason?"

"Olivia, your grandpa told you about this," Miguel answered. "Vivian, your father, Charles's father, and Dash's mother were my best friends. We made up a group called the Blazing Stars. Raven met us when we were about twenty."

Olivia remembered her grandpa had mentioned the Blazing Stars. She felt a pang of guilt when her dad mentioned Raven's name.

"But how does that relate to the Black Death?" Vivian asked.

Miguel sat down on a log. "Agnes was about twenty years old at the time. She's not sixty years old now because she put a stop to her aging. Anyway, Agnes instantly hated us. We wanted to defeat the Black Death, just like you. We tried, but we just didn't have the strength that your children have. I'm sorry to say this, but yes, Agnes killed your parents."

Vivian gasped. Charles and Dash's eyes got wide with extreme surprise and anger.

"And, well, she killed Olivia and Jayden's grandfather too."

She did what? Olivia thought. *HOW DARE SHE!!* Olivia wished she had done something more horrible to the witches. They had tried to destroy her family!

"I'm even happier we killed that devil now," Olivia said. "How dare she!"

Miguel nodded, his eyes darkened with sadness.

"But why didn't she kill you too?" Charles asked.

"Well, Agnes, she...she fell in love with me," Miguel sighed. "Of course, I didn't like her, so that's why she put a love potion on me."

Olivia pieced it all together. *That makes more sense,* she thought. *Dad would never fall in love with someone like Agnes!*

"There's nothing we can do about our parents now," Charles said. He shook his head to refresh his mind. "So we might as well start living in the present."

"We're glad the real you is back, Miguel." Dash grinned. "We were worried."

They happily followed Miguel out of the woods. Suddenly, he collapsed on the ground, shaking and whimpering.

"Dad!" Olivia exclaimed, bending down to him. "What's happening?"

Miguel looked up at her with sadness and pain in his eyes. "I'm sorry, my dear," he breathed, his body unnaturally twisting and turning. "A long time ago, Agnes put yet another spell on me. The spell said that if you defeated her, I would be bewitched and suffer. Then I would die. The time has come for that to happen."

Olivia couldn't believe this was happening—after all her hard work to bring her true family back together. She and her friends had tried so hard to get rid of Agnes, who brought much sadness to their family, but all their effort had only resulted in one last piece of sadness—even more depressing than all that came before.

"Why didn't you tell me?" she asked her dad, tears streaming down her face. "We didn't have to defeat Agnes."

He shook his head with the last ounce of strength he had left in his body.

"I couldn't," he said. "Or else you wouldn't try. But I'm proud you did what you had to. Goodbye! Remember...I will always love you, no matter where I am!"

He took a deep breath, his last, immersing him into the longest sleep possible—a sleep that would last forever.

32

Olivia ran her trembling hand across her dad's pale face. Her tears trickled onto the ground beside them, forming minuscule pools of sadness.

"Why," she whispered. "Why him?" She looked up at the sky. "Why!" Olivia felt her friends wrap around her grieving body as more tears ran down her face. She threw her head back and screamed. She screamed with all her might and flung her backpack off her shoulders.

"Olivia, calm down," Dash soothed, laying his hand on her shoulder.

Olivia shook him off. As if he would understand! He hadn't even known his mother. Here, Olivia had a devilish mom and a deceased father who had meant more to her than she had ever realized. He was always there to support her, ready to bring her forward through all of the tragedies and hard times in her life. When she had success, a happy moment, he would always celebrate with her, sharing the occasion. And he would always be proud of her. She was so angry. Why had she been chosen to suffer through all this? Why?

"Why me!" Olivia screamed. "Why do I have to go through all of this! I thought you loved me, Grandpa! I thought you would protect me! But instead, you chose to torture me, to make me work so hard just to see my dad die in front of my own eyes!"

Olivia turned her back on her friends and ran away from her dad's body. She ran, letting all of the anger in her body rush away into the flowing air. At last, she collapsed on the ground, too tired to run anymore. All of that anger had ebbed away into grief, and she closed her eyes, hoping to never wake into the real world again.

"Olivia," a voice sounded. "Olivia!"

Olivia felt confused as she opened her eyes in bright surroundings. She was in Vivian's bedroom, lying on Vivian's pink bed. Her friends were sprawled across Vivian's fluffy white rug, all with puffed-up red eyes.

Vivian's mom was standing over Olivia, her eyes also wet. *What? Who? Where?* Olivia was so confused and tired. She felt like closing her eyes and going back to sleep, where she could be by herself.

"What happened?" Olivia asked.

Vivian's mom shook her head. "Your father is gone," she said. "But we still have each other."

Olivia looked into her brown eyes, just like Vivian's. *Oh, yes, my dad died,* Olivia thought, angry. *That's what happened!* Vivian's mother seemed extremely sad, overwhelmed by grief for her best friend since childhood. But a hint of happiness in her eyes created a very small spark, even though she tried to hide it. Of course! She was happy because Max had returned home after so many long years.

"Agnes took a huge fortune from your family," Vivian's mother said as Vivian sat beside Olivia. "You and Jayden will come in possession of it when you are of age."

Olivia nodded. She didn't want money. She didn't care for it. She just wanted her dad back.

"Where's Dash?" Olivia asked, wanting to tell him something.

"Dash, over here, honey!" Vivian's mom called. "Olivia has something to say to you."

Dash's disappointed face appeared beside the bed.

Dash had loved Olivia's dad and he must be missing him as well.

"Dash, I'm sorry," Olivia apologized. "I shouldn't have yelled at you in the woods."

Dash nodded, holding back tears. "It's okay," he sniffled. "You were upset."

Charles walked up next to Dash and smiled at Olivia. "We'll always be here for you, you know," he grinned, but with sad eyes as well.

"I know, and I'm so thankful to have friends like you guys." Olivia smiled.

Vivian's mom coughed, jerking PowerSurge back into the present.

"Olivia, you and Jayden will be living with us now," Vivian's mom said.

"I would like that," Max said, looking right at his serious mother. Vivian nodded excitedly, squeezing Olivia's hand.

"Well, then," Vivian's mom said with a grin on her face. "It is settled."

Olivia heard pawsteps and Magnus appeared by her bed. She sat up and gave him a hug as he licked her face. She envisioned her dad and grandpa, sitting side by side as they watched her in the company of her new family. She would always miss her dad, but she knew he had to go. She couldn't have left the witches alive to save him. That would've been the wrong thing to do. She sent a silent prayer to her grandpa, telling him that she didn't mean what she said to him. She would always be best friends with Vivian, Charles, and Dash, no matter what. Her life had totally transformed, now that she had a brother. And Max would always be there for her, ready to do whatever she needed of him. Olivia was fearless now. She had faced the happiness and sadness that life had to offer. She had been through the hard and the easy, the sad and the happy. And she had saved everyone she knew from the Black Death, with the help of her loyal friends.

The memories of her dangerous quest never left Olivia's mind, but from then on, she enjoyed the rest of her precious life with her loving family, treasuring every single moment spent with them.

Acknowledgments

My amazing teacher, Mr. Maskell, for inspiring me to write this book

My supportive mom, for motivating me to publish this book

Mrs. Nancy Cohn, my kindergarten teacher, for helping me enhance my book

Mrs. Jane Kelley, for giving me thoughtful beneficial edits and suggestions

Mrs. Rochelle Melander, for helping me publish the book.

About the Author

Shivani Ganeshan has always dreamed of publishing a story of her own. An avid reader since the age of five, she's been inspired by some of the world's greatest fantasy authors. When she was ten, a fantasy writing unit at school spurred her ideas for *The Sign in the Smoke.* The publishing of this fantasy adventure has made her dream come true.

Shivani has participated in numerous writing competitions and has developed creative writing pieces for newsletters, collaborations, and just for fun! She lives in Chicago with her parents, brother, and her adorable dog, Astro.

CPSIA information can be obtained
at www.ICGtesting.com
Printed in the USA
BVHW071132230521
607950BV00015B/283